Ian Abraham first started characters for the Meean university studying biology b… that period, he was also introduced to healing with crystals and spiritualism. This opened a new doorway of interest and can often be seen in his work too. After leaving, he wrote several pieces to try to find the right fit, but eventually his life was given to the universe he created. During this time, *Eyes of Eternal Souls* was born by a woman's eyes. It tells of various characters, who each have their own unique qualities, which are all derived from Ian's emotions. His writing mostly revolves around commercial fiction. Having suffered abuse as a child from seven years of age and suffered many different things, he has many emotions that are released in the writing.

In recent years Ian suffered a severe head blow, costing him most of his life memories. Now he sees stories all the time. All his writing is done to music. Some artists help to inspire certain moods, but the unknown, dark-haired woman has been his greatest inspiration. A person's eyes are a gateway to their soul. This was true when seeing her eyes, which brought about his favourite character and a future concept. He has always enjoyed stories and his belief is that one exists in everything there is. He has proven this many times by just being presented with a prop and then telling a story about it. Stories have always been something that Ian has enjoyed and often escaped to. His life has also led him to believe in things that most won't, allowing him to see with different eyes.

CW01639251

To the unknown, dark-haired woman in the red dress, whose eyes inspired this work.

Ian Abraham

Marnari Rashna

Eyes of Eternal Souls

Austin Macauley Publishers™
London • Cambridge • New York • Sharjah

Copyright © Ian Abraham 2022

The right of Ian Abraham to be identified as author of this work has been asserted by the author in accordance with sections 77 and 78 of the Copyright, Designs and Patents Act 1988.

All rights reserved. No part of this publication may be reproduced, stored in a retrieval system, or transmitted in any form or by any means, electronic, mechanical, photocopying, recording, or otherwise, without the prior permission of the publishers.

Any person who commits any unauthorised act in relation to this publication may be liable to criminal prosecution and civil claims for damages.

This is a work of fiction. Names, characters, businesses, places, events, locales, and incidents are either the products of the author's imagination or used in a fictitious manner. Any resemblance to actual persons, living or dead, or actual events is purely coincidental.

A CIP catalogue record for this title is available from the British Library.

ISBN 9781398407251 (Paperback)
ISBN 9781398416079 (ePub e-book)

www.austinmacauley.com

First Published 2022
Austin Macauley Publishers Ltd®
1 Canada Square
Canary Wharf
London
E14 5AA

Chapter 1

Budaru was the capital in the known kingdom of Rhutra. It was here that most would aim to come. Hoping that their life would be changed forever, but for the majority, it became a disappointment. So many sought to better themselves and had no idea what to expect. You had to have something to offer. Most didn't, they just turned up and hoped for the best. It was always told to others that it was the city of wonders. Few seldom saw that aspect. You were either part of the city or part of the problem. It was how those who had made it in Budaru referred to those who lived on the streets or infested the slums. The slums had eventually encroached on the city boundaries. Perhaps they should have erected a wall around the main city when they had the chance, but it was too late now. Crime had tripled, but so had the number of unfortunate souls.

It was an old city made mostly of stone and wood. The palace was at the heart of the city. It had originally been fashioned around the palace. This did have a wall to protect it, but when that had been constructed, there had been no city or dwellers in the vicinity it was for the purpose of protection then. Once the king of the land had made a name for himself, the people had flocked here in vast numbers. A city had emerged around it in a matter of years and had grown even more. Eventually, the outer perimeter of the capital had a wall erected. It sort of polished off the city. Those who were looked down upon, were now all a part of the city too. They hoped that by being here, they would be protected. Their lives would improve and they would thrive and prosper. It was not the case. Too many had sought this life, only to find that they were worse off. Most were starving and had taken to thievery to survive. Some would just sit on the streets. The city still had its many visitors and statesman, lords and others who came and went. One of those, who occasionally travelled to the city, was Marnari Rashna. She wore a very colourful cloak and had a hood over to conceal her face. Most knew who she was; well, those of importance. She just chose not to advertise herself to others. The square was erected outside the main pathway to the palace. She was currently walking through there. Steps led her up to the main part of the square. It was a direct route to the palace.

"Hello," came the voice.

It was rare for a civilian to speak to her. Marnari stopped out of curiosity and looked in the direction of the voice. A young girl was stretched out on the raised plinth at the side of the steps. She was sat with her arms supporting her and legs out in front. "It's a nice day, isn't it," she said, with the sun fully on her face.

Marnari would normally have walked on, but there was something intriguing about the girl. She lowered her hood and the girl could see she was a more mature woman, but still pretty with long red hair. The girl was staring at her face.

"Say good morning to the king for me when you see him."

It made Marnari pause for a moment. She was about to resume her walk. "How did you know I was going to see the king?" she asked.

The girl just shrugged her shoulders and Marnari continued to walk away.

"Don't be in such a rush, Bludar. Your wife knows you are safe and on your way home."

Marnari had now reached the centre of the square. Hearing the girl's voice again, she stopped. The king would have to wait. This girl was interesting. Somehow, she knew about others around her.

"Miri and Cari," she called. "You'll be late and in trouble again if you don't hasten your walk."

Marnari returned to the girl.

"Child, what is your name?"

"I am Quinn," she replied.

No one ever asked. It surprised her she had asked, it surprised herself that she could still remember.

"Where do you live?"

"Anywhere I can find. Why?"

So, she was one of the street urchins that the wealthier despised. "Come here," said Marnari.

The girl was unsure why, but got up from where she sat and walked to the end of the plinth. The girl was slender to skinny, probably from lack of food living on the streets. Marnari looked at her eyes and concentrated on them for a brief moment and then she suddenly took a sharp breath from what she had seen there. It even made her take a step back from the girl. This surprised Quinn and she was a little unsure why she had reacted that way.

“Would you meet me here tomorrow, just before the sun rises and the birds start to sing?”

Quinn was unsure why she wanted her to, but she had nowhere else to be and the lady had been the first to have this much conversation with her, ever.

“Sure,” she eventually said.

“Tell me how old are you?” asked Marnari.

“I don’t know,” she replied. “How long has the king been king? I was told I was one when he was crowned.”

“It has been ten years now.”

“Then I guess I am eleven.”

Marnari had seen something and thoughts had come to her. The girl was probably too old for what she had in mind, but what she had seen made her curious. It certainly warranted further investigation.

“I will see you here tomorrow,” said Marnari.

Marnari resumed her walk. She was late for her meeting with the king. Not that it really bothered her. Most of his court looked down on her. They didn’t like what she was, but that didn’t matter. She and the king had known each other since before he had been crowned. So, he rarely listened to them where she was concerned. His message had stated that he needed her council on a matter. She arrived at the palace’s outer wall and was admitted.

One of the king’s advisors entered the throne room. “Your Majesty, the Mystic has arrived.”

“Excellent,” he said.

It would make a change from the dull, boring, mundane routine of the day. Marnari entered.

“Marnari,” he called.

The advisors were not impressed by his behaviour and outburst.

"Your Majesty, it is good to see you. It has been so long since I last saw you."

"Yes, it has. Would you accompany me to the gardens so we can talk?"

It was more a statement than a question as he had already offered her his arm. She took it and went with him. He didn't speak until they were outside. Once, the gardens had been more extensive and lavish, but when the palace wall had to be constructed, a lot of the garden was lost. He had played here as a child. That had been many years ago.

"What did you wish to speak to me about?" asked Marnari, once they were alone.

"I have a delicate situation with Lord Broson in the south. It would seem he has accused one of my advisors of having an affair with his wife. It was asked that I attend personally as it is such a delicate matter, but I am unable to leave at this time. Lord Rhunar is expected tomorrow."

"I see and you believe that he will speak to me?"

He handed her a sealed letter with his personal seal.

"He has no reason not to."

"Now I know why you chose the gardens. Less eyes are watching here," she said. "Hopefully none."

She had also aided his father in the past. There were a few who didn't like that she was referred to as a mystic. It was the former king who had bestowed that title upon her. She found it rather amusing at the time.

"How soon do I need to be there?"

"Can you leave tomorrow?"

"Yes," she said, it was not possible to say no to him.

He was the king, but she had also made arrangements to collect Quinn. Never mind, she would have to accompany her on the journey there. It would serve as well to talk as they travelled.

"Would Your Majesty permit me to have a second horse. I intend to collect someone before dawn as I depart and only have the one horse. As you wish me to go immediately, I will not have time to collect a second."

He laughed.

"Is this a way of me paying for your service to lend you a horse that will never see the inside of a royal stable again?"

"Your Majesty," she said, trying not to smile.

It was obvious his father had told him about the time she had borrowed before. She was still riding it to this day.

"Well, I have an interest in one of the young street urchins. There is something interesting about her so you would actually be giving it to one of your royal subjects. Not I, Your Majesty."

"Fine, fine," he said, still laughing, "then your friend can consider it a gift. I do see that the horse my father gave you is still doing well."

Yes. He was aware.

"At least you can see that I appreciate my gifts from the royal family and I do take very good care of them too," she said.

The two of them were still laughing when they returned to the royal court. He called over one of his squires and whispered in his ear.

"Milady, if you would allow me to escort you to the royal stables?"

She turned and curtsied to the king then departed with the squire. There was still a smile on both of their faces.

When they arrived at the stables, the squire spoke to her.

"His Majesty said you could take any horse you wished."

"Really?"

She was surprised.

"Perhaps you should tell me, which is the king's horse."

"Milady?" Was she intending to take that one?

She saw the look on his face.

"Don't be alarmed, I just wanted to make sure I didn't take it."

"As if that would ever stop you," came a voice.

He remembered whose horse she had borrowed and kept in the past. She turned around. The voice was familiar. He was much older now, but she still recognised him.

"Trudan," she said, greeting him with a hug.

He was the royal stable master. Trudan had also been the stable master in the past, under the former king. She didn't like formalities, probably why some didn't like her in the royal court.

"You can go, squire," he said. "I can look after the lady."

"Well, there are plenty in the palace who would disagree," she said. "Just because they have titles doesn't make them lords and ladies."

She smiled.

"No, it doesn't. So, who is the horse for?" he asked.

"A young lady. I will collect her before dawn in the square."

"I didn't know you knew any ladies," he said.

She smiled at him.

"She is a street urchin who seems to have an interesting gift."

"Ah," he said, he believed he knew who she meant.

"Quinn," she said, hearing the comment.

"Seems to be able to take one look at you and know something about you."

"Yes, I saw it too, which is why I asked if she would like to accompany me from tomorrow. Do you know much about her?"

"I only know she lost her mother and was raised by an old lady. Who then mysteriously left when she was about five? Then the streets raised her, but she was never mean or stole or anything. She told people things about themselves. Always good."

"How did she get by?"

"Kindness of others. Her words have always seemed to put others at ease."

"Interesting."

"What about this horse? It was the king's horse when he was a boy. Would be perfect for her," suggested Trudan.

"He looks fine, but getting old now. What about this one?"

"I don't know if you should take that one," he said.

"Why is that?"

"Well, I am not sure, but I believe it was the horse that belonged to the woman he loved."

"Ah, well then, it will be perfect. Out of sight, out of mind. He can put the past to rest and move on."

She approached the horse and placed a hand on the side of its face. It was pure white, but when she looked at its eyes, the beast looked sad.

"I think she will be perfect for Quinn. You're coming with us," she said to the horse.

It made a sound, almost as if it understood.

"Would you happen to be up early tomorrow?" she enquired.

"I find it is hard to break a habit like that. So, yes."

"Would you be able to bring this horse to the square just before dawn?"

He smiled and nodded.

Quinn was there on time. Considering she had slept in the square overnight. She had been intrigued when the lady had asked if she wished to accompany her. When the two had met, she had looked at the lady's eyes. They were hard to understand. She saw things, but everything was such a mess and a jumble, it was hard to understand anything about her. It seemed she was complicated. Trudan had arrived with the horse. Marnari crouched and shook Quinn's shoulder. She started to stir. "Well, I guess this was one way to ensure you weren't late."

"It's been warm in the nights. I have slept here a lot," said Quinn.

Quinn rubbed her eyes and sat up. Trudan walked over with the horse seeing the two of them. He handed a package to Marnari.

"What's this?"

"I thought they might be more appropriate for the young lady to ride in."

Marnari opened the bundle.

"Thank you."

She handed them to Quinn, who started to strip off there and then.

"Not here," said Marnari. "A young lady should be more dignified. You are travelling with me, remember?"

"My apologies, milady," she said, then ran down an alley and changed behind a barrel.

It was just pants, shirt and jacket, but was much better than the rags she had been wearing. The two of them mounted, although Quinn needed help. She had never ridden before. Before Quinn mounted, she had stared at the horse's face. Then she hugged her around the neck. Trudan had never seen that before. He handed Marnari one last package.

"In case you both get hungry," he said.

"Thank you, Trudan."

The two set off at a trot.

"I bet you intend to name your horse," said Marnari, as they started to leave the city.

"No. She already has one. It's Clara."

"So, how do you know that?"

"She told me."

"When?"

"I saw it in her eyes. She was with a young woman with long fair hair and a white dress, she had a flower in her hair on the right. It was the day she got the horse."

Marnari looked over at her. It was like she had just described someone she had once known.

"What colour was the flower?"

"Pink. She told the prince that its colour resembled love and she loved him very much."

She had thoughts racing through her head, but was unclear about something. The details were similar to what someone else had heard. No. It couldn't be the same woman.

"Let's go," she said, and picked up the pace.

Chapter 2

The two of them arrived at the city of Liptus two days later. Lord Broson was not expecting them. In fact, he was very surprised that the king had not come himself. He didn't much care for the witch. A lot of the lords considered her to be just that. She had been around since the king's father had been on the throne and no one really knew why. She would only do what the king asked. It was strange that he would request her to come. The former king had named her a mystic, but no one could see what was mystical about her. In her youth, she would have been seen as an attraction, but then it was thought the king had certain other interests in the woman, but then he married and she still kept appearing. Only when called though. Now she was here at his court. Broson sent his lowliest of advisors to speak with the wench. She was nothing more than that to him and a lot of others too.

"My Lord."

His advisor was back. The wench wasn't with him so hopefully he had got rid of her. As he looked at the advisor, he was presented a letter. It had the king's seal.

Perhaps she was nothing more than a messenger. He opened it and read the contents.

"Aargh!" he cried. "Why do I have to suffer this? Leave." Now he turned to his chief advisor.

"The king isn't coming, he has Rhunar arriving. You know what to do, proceed to alternative arrangements. Have Sculnar change target. He will be required here tonight. I have to entertain this damn fool mystic."

"Understood."

His first advisor left and the mystic was shown into the assembly room.

"Apologises, Lord Broson. The king thought it was best that I attend. As you know, over the years, I have always been discreet."

She had that. Slipping in and out the kings' quarters at all hours, although no one actually knew the true details. It was nothing more than idle gossip. That had not gone down well with the king when he eventually found out. What he was surprised to see was the young girl with her. That was new. She normally travelled alone. Marnari could see his eyes on her.

"Please excuse the girl. I had hoped to have returned home, but the king insisted that I attend to your needs first."

The two sat opposite him and began to talk about the situation at hand. What Marnari was not aware was that it was merely a ruse, designed to get the king to the lord. Quinn sat and looked around the room. She had nothing else to do so decided to see what was there. She had only known the capital, so it didn't hurt to see how others lived. As she looked, her attention was not on the conversation. Then something was said. That made no sense and then she looked at Lord Broson. It was the first time she had taken a close look at him. What that meant is, it was the first time she had looked into his eyes. When she looked, it worried her. She placed a hand on Marnari's arm. She needed to speak to her, but didn't want to interrupt; she knew that would be wrong. Even for someone on the streets, she had been an observer of people and had learned how they treated each other and also when and when not to speak. Timing was everything.

Marnari felt the hand on her, but had to ignore it. The hand remained for a while longer. Then Quinn got up and started to walk around the room. She quietly moved.

Almost as if she wasn't there. Then the strangest thing happened. One minute she had been on one side of the room and then moved to another. The crashing of a vase hitting the floor came from where she had been, not where she was. Lord Broson was immediately up from his seat, thinking it was an intruder. Marnari also went to rise, but her arm was grabbed by Quinn.

"We need to leave," she started to say. "We are in danger."

Lord Broson was leaving the broken vase and returning to his seat. Marnari had no time to ask what she meant, but she sensed concern in the girl and if she was right, her gift meant she was unable to lie.

"Faint," she whispered.

Marnari sat and resumed the conversation with Lord Broson. He blamed the crash on an open window. Quinn was unsure if she had heard correctly or not. She was sure she had heard her say 'faint', but why? She had continued to walk the room. Then it struck her as to what she was implying.

"Oh, my," said Broson. "The girl has collapsed."

Marnari turned at his outburst and then rushed to Quinn.

"My Lord, I do believe the journey had been too much for her. It was stressed that it was so urgent to see you that we chose not to rest on the journey. I should have realised that the girl was not cut out for such a task."

Quinn was quite light and Marnari had no problem scooping her up her arms. "Is there somewhere that she can rest?"

Lord Broson went to the door and called for a guard. He instructed him to take her to one of the guest quarters. As he re-entered the assembly hall, he was met by Sculnar.

"My Lord, I understand there is a change of target?"

"Yes. Kill the mystic and the girl. It should be easy; the girl has just fainted and Marnari is distracted right now."

"Understood, I will send my men now."

Marnari was busy listening to what Quinn was trying to tell her. "Stop, take a deep breath and then let it out very slowly," she said. Quinn did as instructed.

"He is intending to kill the king. That's why he wanted him here as it was easier. I could see it in his eyes. The most recent activity is usually the easiest to read."

"We have to get back to the palace so we can warn them," said Marnari.

"Nope. We have to prepare to save ourselves first," said Quinn.

"What do you mean?"

"We came in error and he doesn't like you."

Marnari smiled, "Not many do."

There was then a knock at the door. Quinn lay down and shut her eyes, just in case Lord Broson had returned. As Marnari opened the door, she was very roughly thrown backwards into the room. They were armed and drew their weapons. Marnari quickly got to her feet.

"Vreshna," she said and moved her arms outwards.

The guards were thrown away from her. Quinn had heard that word before and knew it.

"Don't hurt them," she called, as she grabbed the nearby drink and threw the contents of water up into the air.

Then she twirled her hand underneath. Marnari was fascinated by her actions and was also familiar with something similar. Then Quinn was dancing around on the dusty floor, her feet scuffing across its surface. The twirl of her hand had separated the water and it became droplets, but something else had happened to it too as it was only slowly descending to the ground. As she danced more, the dust from the floor started to rise upwards. The guards were slowly gaining their composure and picking up their weapons. Marnari was not concerned about them. She could very easily deal with them all with a snap of her fingers. This is why the king had always sought her out. Marnari was more interested in Quinn. The guards were up and moving towards them. She stopped dancing instantly then clapped her hands one over the other. One up, one down. The dust and the water droplets merged and as soon as they did, Quinn moved her hands outwards. The droplets hit the guards in their eyes and the dust started to irritate them. Quinn didn't hesitate, even if Marnari had. She grabbed her hand and pulled her through the open door. Marnari came to her senses as soon as Quinn had pulled on her hand.

"Why didn't you want them hurt?"

It had been puzzling her.

"They only followed orders. Like when the guards chase the beggars off the streets. It's just an order they have to follow."

More guards were following them and they still had to get their mounts. There was no time to learn more. They had to move quickly.

Once they were on approach to the stable, Quinn did something else that was strange too. "CLARA," she called.

It was as if the horse knew why it was being called. Moments later, the two horses appeared. Fortunately, the stable hands here were lazy and they still had saddles. The two mounted and raced out of the courtyard. Guards were trying to follow, but had been unprepared for the horses.

Now they were clear of the city, they could ease up on the horses; they would not have the strength to gallop all the way back to Budaru.

"Do you know what you did back there?"

"Yes."

She didn't even pause or try to hide it.

"I heard you speak and knew it was safe. I don't like to hurt people. So, I learned what I call gentle magic."

"There is no such thing."

"Yes, there is, and I just proved it back there."

That was one thing she couldn't argue. She had seen that type of magic once before. When she had been training. The woman who had taught her had shown her an alternative to destructive magic. Marnari had not found it to be effective, but Quinn had been able to disable the guards. It wasn't something that could work every time and her dance had made her actions slow. If she wasn't careful, she could very well get herself killed.

They had no choice, but to keep going. It was dark and the roads were treacherous. Quinn leaned forward and spoke into Clara's ear.

"What did you say?" asked Marnari.

"I said I hope you know the way to the king as I'm lost."

"Have you always been able to do that?"

"Do what?" asked Quinn.

"Speak to animals and have them understand?"

"I don't know about animals, but horses tend to understand me. The old lady told me I had what she called 'insight'."

"This old lady, what was she like?"

"Old."

"Describe her."

"She had white hair. Old and wrinkled, but not bent over or unable to get about. She was still capable of doing things for herself and no one disrespected her, otherwise she would tell them off."

Marnari smiled. She sounded like an interesting woman. "How did you come to be with the old woman?"

"She told me that she had been asked to look after me, but a few years later, she just vanished and never came back. I was still very young and didn't know what to do, but then I started to see things in people's eyes and say nice things to them. They took pity on me and gave me food and stuff."

"If you were still young, when did you learn the gentle magic?"

"She was teaching me things from the first moment I could speak. I guess as you need words for some magic, it was pointless before."

That was true, although she had been able to use her art without words. It had been really interesting to see, but knew that she would need a lot of help to learn other things too. Her insight had been right when the two of them had first met. Quinn was special. The question was, how special?

They arrived at Budaru the next morning. There was a lot of activity. Marnari didn't stop and continued to ride through the city. She and Quinn were eventually stopped when they arrived at the square. Something had definitely happened.

"I need to see the king," she said.

"No one is allowed admittance."

"You do realise who I am, don't you?" she started to say.

Quinn tugged at her arm. The guard was then busy with the next person. Still holding her arm, she led her down a side street and several alleys.

"Where are we going, Quinn?"

"To the palace."

"This is not the way in."

She glanced back and smiled.

"Depends really, doesn't it. The front is for one type of person, the back is for another." She walked to the rear entrance. The tradesman entrance. There was only a single guard here.

"'Ere to see stable master Trudan, guv'nor," said Quinn.

"Your business with him?" he asked.

"Well, if you won't let me see him to confirm the king's orders, that he came by to place with the blacksmith the other day, then I guess I had better leave or you can summon him quick, guv'nor?"

Marnari was really intrigued. She had held back like Quinn had asked.

"Come on," she said. "I ain't got all day, there's a piece of bread in this for me."

Marnari was starting to smile. The guard left and Trudan returned with him. He was unsure what all the commotion was about. He had only just confirmed an order with the blacksmith. Then he saw Quinn and realised what was going on.

"It's fine, guard."

The guard left him to speak to the girl.

"Where is Marnari?"

"Here," she said, stepping from the shadows.

He sighed with relief.

"I am here to warn the king Lord Broson intends to kill him. We came back as fast as we could."

He ushered them through the gate.

"You're too late; it happened late last night."

"What? It was supposed to happen at Liptus, that was why he summoned the king so he could make it easier to kill him."

"Well, he found a way, that's why no one is allowed in. Rhunar was injured in the attack. He tried to save the king, but alone he wasn't enough. The immediate guards had already been dealt with; it took some time for others to get to them. By then it was already too late."

"So, what now?" asked Marnari.

Trudan was looking at her, but his mouth wasn't working. Quinn looked at him. Then gasped. Trudan had forgotten that she could do that.

"Tell me or she will."

He paused, still hesitating.

"Speak," said Marnari.

"It was rumoured some years ago that the reason the king kept the horse you took was more than a reminder of the woman he had loved. It was said it was for his child."

"What?" said Marnari. "Why didn't she stay?"

"Apparently she wasn't of royal linage."

"So, who is she and did she have the child or what?"

"It is unclear."

"How do we find out? There has to be someone who might know."

Quinn was still looking at Trudan's eyes.

"Stop that," he said.

"No," she said. "You have seen many things."

He closed his eyes. Marnari looked at Quinn.

"All I got was a name. Does Crellis mean anything to you?"

Trudan opened his eyes.

"Damn you, child."

"Stop it, Trudan. She cannot help her gift and you shouldn't hold out on me at a moment like this."

Crellis had been the former king's General, but had left his service. Not long after he died, but it was unclear why.

"Now I have one more question. Please don't hold out on me again, otherwise I might start to think we aren't friends."

"It's nothing to do with that. With everything that is happening, anyone could be listening and you are stood here prying secrets from me that could get the heir killed. Quinn, look into my eyes and take what you need, but say nothing until you are far from the city. Do you understand the importance of this?"

She nodded then looked. After a moment, she said thank you. Now, she took Marnari's hand and led her back to the square. Trudan had disappeared. It was too risky to be out of the palace. He hoped that they would both be safe.

Chapter 3

They mounted their horses, who hadn't moved since being forced to dismount. Now Quinn leaned forward and whispered to Clara. She started off at a slow trot. Marnari didn't say anything. She knew why Quinn was whispering. They rode out of town and had to stop at a local tavern for the night. Marnari looked at Quinn when they had stopped. All she did was shake her head. She could hear the whispers in the next room. She knew enough not to speak about where they were going. It had surprised her when she saw it in his eyes. Quinn had heard of it, but believed it a mere tale, told by travellers.

The next day, they set off before dawn. Quinn was up and wanting to leave early. They had a lot of people staring at them when they arrived. She didn't like that, maybe she was becoming paranoid. Nevertheless, they left. She whispered to Clara again. It was several miles later before Marnari considered they were alone. The trees of the forest had passed the road was empty and the land was open and flat. No one could be seen for miles.

"So, are you going to tell me or do I have to wait until we get there?"

"When I saw, I didn't believe it even existed," said Quinn.

"What do you mean?"

"Tel'd'shar."

Marnari stopped her horse.

"Please tell me that was a joke."

Quinn stopped and looked back.

"No."

"Do you realise where Tel'd'shar is?"

"No."

"Do you know anything else other than that word?"

"Yes, but that would not be the correct answer," said Quinn.

"There are only two ways to get there. The first is by boat," said Marnari and then stopped.

"The other?" asked Quinn.

"They call it the gateway."

"Another story told by travellers."

"It is no story."

"Have you been there then?"

"Once."

"Well, I don't want to leave Clara behind. If the gateway means no boat, then we will go that way."

Marnari didn't like the idea of that, but if they were to find the truth, they had to find Crellis.

"It is not something we should attempt."

"Why?" asked Quinn.

"The gateway is in the land of the Vilhar."

"I haven't heard of them."

"They live in what is now called the dead forest. It spans the whole of the north-eastern boundary."

"Does nothing grow there then?" she asked.

"It is called the dead forest, because all that go there are killed, by the Vilhar."

"Oh. Are they bad people then?" Quinn was full of questions.

"They didn't use to be then something changed. It is a long ride."

"I would like to meet the Vilhar."

"You are a strange one, Quinn."

"How do we get there?" asked Quinn, still continuing with the questions.

"I guess you will have to follow me?"

They turned at the next crossroads and took the road east.

"How long will it take us to get there?" asked Quinn, after they had been riding for about two hours.

"A few days."

She looked across, surprised. "Really!"

"Yes. It isn't like walking through the capital and getting to where you want in a few moments. Have you never travelled before?" asked Marnari.

"No. Well, all I can remember is the city. If I have come from somewhere else, then I was too young to realise."

"I think I can now understand why you want to meet and see all these things that are getting mentioned. You have a curious nature."

"Don't you?" asked Quinn.

"Not as much as I used to. These eyes have seen too much over the years."

"I see a lot. Especially when I look into someone's eyes."

"I have to ask. Have you ever looked into my eyes?"

"Yes. When we met. I do it with everyone."

"Oh," now Marnari was surprised. "What did you see?"

"A mess," came the reply.

It wasn't what she had expected.

"What do you mean a mess?" asked Marnari.

"Your eyes show so many things that it is hard to tell what is linked to this, that or something else."

"So far, I have seen the king, his father, a partial thought when I first mention what I saw with Clara, a memory of the General. Even Trudan, but I don't get one thing at time. All images from your eyes come rushing forward. Like I said, a mess."

She was honest, sometimes blunt, but she never sugar-coated it. Marnari guessed that it was just her way and she needed to understand that.

They would need to find somewhere to stay overnight. Quinn was going to have to get used to things taking longer than a walk. This would be a long journey. It would seem that there was much that Quinn didn't know about the real world, but she seemed to know plenty about others' worlds. The next day, they had to cross the Durian plains. They were named that from the beast that roamed the lands; although, over the centuries that had passed since its naming, most of these beasts had been slaughtered for food. They were a good source of food and non-violent. Very easy to catch or kill. With that in mind, they were sought after from all over the land. It wasn't believed that any wild beasts existed anymore, but it had retained its name upon the land where once they roamed. Now it was a dusty, dry area. Hot, arid and dry. The land had little growth there now. The Nirris river that once ran through the area had been diverted a long time ago and the land failed to get sufficient rain to maintain any flora or fauna. However, it was still the fastest route to the east. They would have to go east before going into the dead forest. There was a mountain range that towered across the land, slicing away at the terrain and leaving the north east cut off from the rest of the kingdom. The Vilhar preferred it that way. You had to enter the forest from the southernmost point of the range. There were those who had been able to cheat by going over the range, but for most attempting that, it had cost them dearly. The air was so thin and icy cold that so few actually survived. It was said there was a thin narrow pass somewhere within the range that allowed for travel, but the whereabouts of its entrance had been lost so long ago that no one even tried to find it anymore. The Vilhar basically lived there alone. It was said if you were tired of life and cared not how it ended, then go to the dead forest. The Vilhar would be glad to oblige. Now their journey was to take them that way. It was very hot for the two of them, and took all day to cross. They had to ensure they had plenty of provisions for themselves and their mounts. When Marnari had asked at the inn for extra food and water, they enquired why. She then told them her route. They considered her and the girl to be mad. No one travelled that way anymore. It was a place where you were likely to die from the heat. The two of them had their heads wrapped. It was hot, but at least they didn't burn from the heat. There was no shelter, no shade. Just the dust and that only seemed to move into the air as they rode. It would seem that not even the breeze would grace the land with its presence. The horses couldn't be pushed either. It was hard enough at a trot. To race across in hope of getting to the other side would only exhaust them. This land was worse than trying to cross a desert. At least there you would eventually find an oasis. There wasn't even one of those here.

They reached the grasslands on the other side. Marnari was familiar with the area. It wasn't the first time for her to pass across the plains. There was a river not too far away, which is why she had insisted upon a particular route. She knew where they would arrive.

"Get refreshed. Let the horses drink, but only enough to quench their thirst."

"Why?" asked Quinn.

"This is bandit country. We will need to use their speed if we encounter trouble."

"I thought the king dealt with bandits and stopped their behaviour?" Quinn wondered.

"His hand might be great, but even he has limits as to how far he can reach. To the south is the route that takes you to Hygredon. East is bandit country until you reach the river Tarji. On the other side is the way to Preteshae. There is a port there that will take you to the land of others."

"Who?" asked Quinn.

"Another time, I am tired and need to rest before we move forward. I suggest you rest too. The horses will alert us if there is trouble."

They had only been resting about an hour when both the horses started to neigh and it only became more persistent. Clara butted Quinn to wake her. Then Marnari was up too.

"We have company. Move now," she whispered.

The two mounted as quickly as they could. There was very little time to determine the correct route to where Marnari wanted to go, but right now, they had to go. A band of cut throats and thieves were running across the land. They had to hope the horses were well-rested. They set off at a gallop.

Quinn had gotten better at his, but was still new to galloping. She had to place her trust in Clara, but the leaps across the ground were making it hard for her to stay straight in her saddle. All she wanted to do right now was lean forward and wrap her arms around Clara's neck. Marnari pushed her horse hard and Clara was aiming to keep up. She didn't need to ask Clara to go faster. It was like she understood the urgency and did what was necessary. Quinn made the mistake of looking back as Clara made a small leap forward. She bounced in the saddle and then the next thing she knew she was bouncing on the ground. She was glad for the long pants as it made it easier to run, but both horses were gone and she was alone. They had almost made it to the trees though. The bandits were chasing hard and fast they would be on her in moments. Then…

There was an almighty roar. It came echoing out of the trees. Quinn stopped and Marnari turned to see what was happening. It was only now that she realised that Quinn was in trouble. She started to run back and then she saw it—him. Whatever the thing was! It was over seven feet tall and carrying what most would have called a staff, but its length was taller than the beast and the thickness of the staff resembled something close to a thin tree. He saw Quinn running towards his direction. He lumbered forward, what most called a run. The staff slid along his hand, the bandits were close. Then he swung the staff and stepped past Quinn. The tip connected with several of the bandits. The thickness of the staff and the force with which it was being moved cleaved open the first two's heads. Like an apple being slammed on a rock. One tried to grab it, thinking it would be easier only to be knocked across the field. Those who had not yet reached them had stopped and turned. The beast stopped and turned around to see Quinn.

She was still stood there. He was curious why she hadn't run. Marnari was unsure what to do right now. Quinn could see more clearly than anyone else and didn't see the beast that others did. She looked up at his eyes.

"Thank you," she said. "I am Quinn. It was good of you to help me. I hope I get to return the favour one day. I have to go though, my friend awaits."

He looked across and saw Marnari. Then he turned back to Quinn. "Jugra'li."

"It's nice to meet you, Jugra'li."

Again, Marnari was surprised at Quinn's actions. Eventually, there would come a point when her actions would not surprise her anymore, but it was still new to her. "I am glad you are safe. I thought the beast would hurt you."

Quinn looked over at Marnari, surprised with the use of her words. "He is not a beast. Jugra'li saved me."

"Sorry, I meant that…"

"I know what you meant and you used your words as you meant to say them. You judged without knowing. Perhaps, next time when you see a beast, you will look properly first."

She had just been put in her place by a child, but she was right. If she had been stood in front of it, then maybe she would have been able to see more. Quinn was definitely different. She would see the world through her eyes and by looking at others. Now, they needed to find out where they were, she was sure they had come hurtling in the wrong direction. She needed to get to the other side of the trees to be certain. This was a dangerous country; another reason why travellers chose not to cross the plains. Still, they were making good time, even with the complications.

Chapter 4

They were travelling in the wrong direction.

"I knew it. I just knew it," said Marnari, annoyed with herself.

"What?" asked Quinn.

"We are heading south, not north. I dare not attempt to retrace our steps, it will take too long."

"Where are we going then?" asked Quinn.

"To the southern fishing port. Hopefully, there is a ship that can take us north."

"Could we not get a ship to Tel'd'shar?" asked Quinn.

"The seas around the point are too treacherous and have so many storms that no one will travel that route. If you wanted to go by ship, we should have just gone straight north and caught one, but you don't want to leave Clara behind."

"Will we have to at the fishing port?"

It concerned her. The thought of having to leave her behind. She was a nice horse with a good soul and kind heart. Having looked into her eyes, she liked what she saw and knew that Clara could be trusted to take care of her. Well, she had one fall, but that was her fault. Nonetheless, she would be sad if she had to leave her behind.

"Maybe."

"Won't you miss your horse? It did belong to a king once."

"My horse is different. It will find me no matter what and if I have to travel by sea and are away too long, it will go home."

"Really? It is that well-trained?"

"Yes."

"It wouldn't accidentally go back to the palace then?" asked Quinn.

"Not yet."

Marnari should have been used to the questions. There were just so many, but then the child had only ever known the capital. It was hard to blame her for that. Since the disappearance of her mentor, Marnari had mostly been on her own. It was hard being around others at times. That needed to change and certainly would now that she had elected to take Quinn with her. Eventually, she would calm. There were only so many questions you could ask. Well, she hoped there were.

They headed south and reached the plains that then led to the forest that skirted around the southern region. The road was clear that passed through it. She had not been this way in many years. So, it was unclear if the bandits had reached this far yet. The two were only travelling at a trot. Marnari had wanted to rest the horses again, just in case their speed was needed. As they started to clear the trees, there was a cart that had lost a wheel and was leaning to one side. The loose apples that had been piled in the back had spilled and were rolling across the dirt road.

"Oh, dear," said Quinn, "perhaps we should stop and help."

Before Marnari could stop her, she had leapt off Clara and ran forward. Marnari had stayed seated and was watching the trees. She had seen similar tricks in other areas.

"Would you like some help?" asked Quinn.

"Certainly," he said turning and drawing a dagger.

Quinn took a step back and started to move her hands at her sides. It was weird as she had nothing in them, but it resembled picking something and throwing it forwards. It took a few seconds, but the apples on the ground seemed to come to life as they jumped up and towards the thief. As she moved her hands faster, the apples on the road moved faster.

Marnari had been right to be concerned. Quinn had made things awkward though. She was surprised at her arm movements; they resembled something else she had seen before. Other thieves dropped from the trees and started to move on the wagon. Quinn was outnumbered and would be surrounded if she didn't remount quickly.

"So, you think to take my target?" came the voice. "I've been tracking them since before the forest and you band of scum think you can steal from me."

Everyone was watching. He had stepped out from behind the trees, an arrow pointed at the group of thieves. Then, it was like he spied something in one of the trees. "You think you can outsmart me?"

He fired and then everyone heard a thud as a body fell from the tree and hit the ground. The thieves had no idea who had just been shot; it wasn't one of theirs and they had no intention of being caught between two other groups of thieves, so they legged it. The cart was abandoned. Not that it mattered, it had been stolen anyway. When they were out of sight, he lowered his bow. It had never been aimed at Quinn or Marnari. She had noticed that he was only interested in the thieves. Quinn had shot across the woods towards the one that had fallen. A fair-haired girl emerged.

Quinn couldn't see an arrow wound anywhere on her.

"You okay, sis?" the other one called.

"That's and interesting way to get rid of the thieves," said Marnari, once the ruse was realised.

"It helps. They have moved too close to the town and people are getting worried. My sister and I decided someone needed to help out. No one else would."

"How long have you been doing this?" asked Marnari.

"A few months."

"What happens when the thieves get wise to your tricks and eventually trap you?" asked Marnari.

"It hasn't happened yet."

He was a little too sure of himself. That wasn't a good thing. From talking to them, they learnt that both of them came from the fishing town they were heading for. He offered to accompany them. Marnari didn't need his assistance. She knew exactly where to go. However, Quinn had engaged in conversation with his younger sister. Both were adults, although it looked like his sister only just made it. She was unsure about them both; they were playing a dangerous game. Quinn hadn't really spoken to many other people and it saved her from answering any questions. They were Riena and Rutar. It didn't take Quinn long to work things out.

The fishing town was larger than expected. It looked relatively clean, as towns go. The streets were cobbled and they had some form of drainage channels at the edges. The brickwork was very dull and dark. Rutar said they came from the dark clays in the southern lands and was traded to them. It made the town look very bleak, but she couldn't fault that it gave a reasonable presentation.

Rutar led them both to the nearest inn. It was strange when they excused themselves. They headed back the way they had come. Marnari wasn't even sure if they had a home to go to. Marnari and Quinn entered the inn. She needed to see if there was a room available then she would need to enquire at the docks for a ship. "Name?" said the innkeeper.

"Why?" asked Marnari.

"So that I can register it in the book."

"You don't seem to have many customers so why does it matter?"

"Find somewhere else then."

He was very rude and unobliging. There probably wasn't another inn for miles.

"Fine. Marnari Rashna and Apprentice Quinn."

Quinn looked up at Marnari. An apprentice, was she really? Is that why she asked her to accompany her? They had never spoken about why she had asked her to accompany her. It had also escaped Quinn to question why too. Right now, though, it would have to wait. The two of them needed to freshen up.

Marnari left Quinn to sort herself out and went down to the docks.

"Excuse me," she said to the first person she saw there.

He looked up, but didn't speak.

"I was wondering if someone had a boat or ship that went to the northern port."

"Earl," he said, nothing more.

"Where is Earl?" asked Marnari.

It really was hard work at this town.

"You won't get much help out of folks around here."

Marnari looked over her shoulder; a youngish man sat on a spool of rope. She glanced him up and down. He was well armed and also carried a pack with him.

Probably a traveller, but one who knew the roads and highways in this area were dangerous.

"Have you been trying to get passage somewhere?" she asked.

"Yes. Same place as you, been here a week and still looking for Earl."

"Does no one know who he is or just too stubborn and lazy to help a traveller out?"

"Well I have wondered that myself. I was set upon before coming here so lost my mount. The only way I can get back to Uboria is to travel by sea. The roads are not safe on foot," he said.

"Are you from Uboria?"

"My uncle is there. I am hoping he will offer me a home. My mother was the last, his sister, she died recently, so the farm has no way of staying stable."

"You know how to handle that?" she inquired, seeing the sword.

"Well enough to get to town. My father used to be in the king's service. He was killed in the west."

"Ah. The Redayans."

"So, you are familiar with that situation?"

"I have aided two kings so far."

"I am Tullan."

"Marnari Rashna," she responded.

"The king's mystic," he said. "My father mentioned such a woman. Was said to be able to charm the former king."

"Ah, I see you have heard those misleading tales. My mentor served him first, but then disappeared. I was then elected to take her place. It is usually mentor and apprentice."

"Didn't there used to be a full order of mystics? At least, that is what my father said."

"Maybe," was all she said.

There indeed had been more of their order, but that was well before her time. The order had shrunk and divided, the great war in the Rhutran continent had taken them apart. The Krykarins were a vicious and blood-thirsty people. It was said that they had wanted to rid the world of them. They worshipped darker arts and so eventually a war had raged for centuries. It was the destruction of the order that eventually put a stop to the war. The Krykarins considered they had won and continued their ways. That was the story that had been told. The reality of what really happened was another thing. No one from the other continents dared travel there. Some of the smaller realms in the smaller continents that existed in the southern hemisphere still suffered even now. Rhutra was the kingdom in the central continent. Tel'd'shar was the capital on the northern continent. Another existed east, but the western ocean only held a small series of islands. There was no continent or kingdoms there. The east, like the north, was a single mass of land. The east was hot and warm the north was its opposite, from cold to icy the further you travelled.

"Considering you're the king's mystic, then perhaps you should start making some noise with the Alcalde that runs this town."

It was an interesting thought.

"Do you happen to know the way?"

Tullan led the way, it was back in the centre of the town. She entered the building and enquired after the Alcalde.

"He is out at present."

"I am the king's mystic and seeking passage to the north. The only response I get is Earl, which seems to lead me nowhere. I need a ship. I am under orders from the king himself."

The Alcalde's advisor was unsure how to respond to that, it was probably easier to address the subject of Earl.

"He is a drunk and will no doubt be in the dock tavern, drunk as he usually is every day. That is why you got no response. His ship is the northern one. Occasionally, he will be asleep there."

"Thank you," she said and left.

On their way back through the centre of town, she bumped into Quinn.

"I came looking for you."

Then she spied Tullan.

"This is Tullan, he needs a ship north too."

"I am Apprentice Quinn," she said to him.

"No, you are just plain Quinn."

"But you said Apprentice Quinn at the inn."

"That was to make us look important."

"Am I, or aren't I?" she asked.

Tullan was slightly behind Marnari and gave a quick nod.

"I saw that," said Marnari. "Tell me what you are an apprentice of."

"I don't know, you haven't said yet."

"Because I haven't decided yet," said Marnari.

"Where are you going now?"

"To the tavern on the docks."

"I'm coming too," said Quinn.

"No, it's a tavern."

"Yes, I am your apprentice and I won't learn if I don't follow you."

"She has you there," said Tullan.

"See, he agrees and he thinks I'm an apprentice too."

"Really?"

"Yes, his eyes tell you already told him."

He looked at Marnari, puzzled.

"She is able to read a person's soul when looking into their eyes. The more recent events are first. The longer she looks, the deeper she can go. It's my understanding. She has a rare and unique gift."

"Interesting. I have never heard of anyone like that before," said Tullan, as they walked.

Quinn was behind and listening. It was a good way to learn things.

Chapter 5

They entered the tavern. It didn't take long to work out which one was Earl. He was the one with his head on the table. Sleep and very drunk. Tullan and Marnari approached the table at the back of the tavern. Quinn hovered at the door.

"You can't come in here," said the innkeeper, seeing her.

"She is with me. That's my apprentice," said Marnari.

"Apprentice? For what?"

"I'm a physician," she continued. "The Alcalde has made a request for this one to be dealt with."

"It's about time. I'm sure he thinks he lives here," commented the innkeeper.

"Then I would like you to stop serving him."

"You don't want that. At least when he's drunk and out cold like that, he isn't trying to pick fights or smash the place up," said the innkeeper.

"Quinn. Will you assist, please?"

While Quinn walked over, she asked Tullan to lift up his head and hold him in position.

"What are you intending?" he asked.

"I need Quinn to read his soul."

Quinn sat opposite him and when she was ready, Marnari opened his eyes. She sat for a moment. He was very drunk and his soul was in torment. It was hard to get a fix on any one thing right now. Quinn waited and waited. It was a long time. Tullan thought he would throw up with the stench of the man. Seems he didn't know how to wash either.

"It would seem he lost someone close to him," said Quinn.

"A daughter," came the voice, from the innkeeper.

It was hard to have a conversation in the tavern without him hearing. Marnari stood up.

"Perhaps then you would like to explain the reason for his condition. I can't help if I don't understand."

Tullan had put his head back down and took Quinn to get some fresh air.

"It would seem she was killed some time ago. At least, that is what is believed. These waters are not safe anymore and Krykarins sometimes stray this way. Every now and then, they take slaves. He was there and couldn't prevent what happened; his ship was set upon. The crew was slaughtered. His daughter was below decks, so it's said. Earl was blind drunk. This is why no one sails with him anymore. He blames his ways for losing her."

"But he is still drunk?"

"So that he doesn't remember anything."

"And when he is sober?"

"Have never seen that yet. As soon as he wakes, he drinks. The cycle is the same every day."

"Well, no more. I need him sober regardless of his condition. Is there anyone who would be willing to carry him to his ship before he wakes?" she asked.

"I know a few, but it will cost."

She took out several coins from a pouch she had and placed them on the counter. "I assume that will suffice."

He was surprised. It was more than enough. Either she had no concept of buying a service or wanted to ensure it got done. The innkeeper was a strong person. For what she had just put on the counter, he had no intention of asking around; he would do it himself. Marnari left to find the others.

"Sorry," said Tullan. "The air was just too bad. I had to escape."

"I have arranged for him to be taken to his ship. I would like to see what condition it is in."

"You know something about ships and sailing them?" inquired Tullan.

"No. I need to ensure he won't escape. I have to get him sober."

The three of them spent the rest of the day ensuring that his cabin was free of any objects that could enable him to affect an escape. Then, Marnari cast a spell on the windows so that they wouldn't open. Well, at least the large ones. The place needed fresh air. It stunk too. His cabin was almost bare, just a bed, chair and table remained. The cabinets were part of the ship's fixings so had to stay. The door was altered and re-fashioned so he could not access the lock from the inside.

It was several hours later that the innkeeper arrived with Earl over his shoulder. He had waited until there were no patrons and then shut up shop. Marnari wasn't surprised to see him on his own. Coin had a way of talking to people and she had ensured her coin was shouting.

"Where do you want him?" he asked.

"In his cabin," said Marnari.

The innkeeper was surprised to see it so tidy and a barrel was on the deck with all of his weapons and things that could have allowed him to get out.

"Thank you," she said, as he left.

Quinn had vanished while they had been sorting out the ship and was just now returning. When she had looked into Earl's eyes, she had seen many things. The walk allowed her to achieve several things. One was to un-jumble what she had seen. The second was to acquire some flowers. Marnari saw her return and was intrigued.

"You said you were a physician and I was your apprentice. I thought I might as well play the part well. On our way into town, I noticed an apothecary, so I went to visit." She carried two types of flowers with her, the first was several bunches of lavender that she asked for help to place them around the room. She needed the scent to help cleanse the atmosphere and act as a secondary aid to the other flower. The other flower was taken from a cananga tree, it was called ylang-ylang. Quinn then placed them on the bed around his head. She had three flowers in total. Now she moved her hands around his head and the flowers, and a mist seemed to form. She now used that to distil and extract the oils from the flowers. The vapours swirled around Earl's head. He would sleep for a considerable time.

"He should be fine until morning."

Marnari had decided to stay on the ship in another cabin. She told Quinn to go back to their room at the inn for the night. To ensure their belongings were safe. Tullan said he would stay on the ship. Earl might wake and become enraged.

The morning came and so did the sun. It rose up over the horizon and blessed the land with its warmth. Quinn was up and about too. She had brought what she could carry from the inn. There was no point paying for a room when the ship was free. It took her several trips to bring everything. After all, wasn't it what an apprentice was supposed to do? She knew that Earl wouldn't be awake yet. Her method and a little magic would ensure he would be well rested and hopefully sober too.

"What damn fool idiot has locked me in here?" came the cries.

Quinn was just returning with the last of the items and saw Earl at the barred windows. It had no glass.

"I did," she said.

Putting the things down she walked over, but not too close. His breath was horrendous.

"Let me out."

"No."

He started to rattle the door his hands almost turning white as he gripped the bars. Earl was strong. Many years on a ship had made it so.

"Stop," said Quinn. "If you want breakfast, behave."

"What do you think I am, a child?"

"Well, you behave worse than I do and I am a child. So, yes."

He stopped and looked at her. What he was trying wasn't working.

"How about you let Earl out so he can have a drink at the tavern," he said.

"No. The innkeeper will not serve you anymore. Besides, you're in there because I need your help."

Marnari and Tullan had been watching; they had appeared hearing the noise, but Earl was unable to see them. The two of them had allowed the conversation to play out. It certainly looked like he couldn't escape. Quinn offered him a piece of fruit. His body had not had food in sometime. All he had tasted for a long time was ale.

"Let me out or so help me, when I get out, I will…"

"Will what? Would you be this mean and nasty to Alara if she was here?"

Marnari assumed that was the name of his daughter.

"I mean, you gave up on her. Is that why she isn't here, because you were so mean and nasty to her?" continued Quinn.

Earl wanted to rip the door open, but his strength was going. It had been a very long time since anyone had ever had the courage to say her name. Let alone stand up to him. His hands left the bars and vanished inside. Earl stepped back and slumped into the chair at the table. He looked sad. Quinn was now looking at him through the bars. Then she unlocked the door. Marnari went to move to stop her, but she had already stepped inside.

When she and Tullan reached the door, she was stood with her hand on his rough greying beard. His mop of hair all long and shaggy, from never being cut in so long. "You know she might still be alive in the east region," said Quinn.

He looked up; she could see the tears in his eyes. Earl was trying too hard to hold them back. Being drunk, he never felt anything. Now he was dealing with all of his emotions at once.

"Please leave," he said.

"I will be outside," Quinn said, "but I have to lock you in again. I really need your help to get to the north. It's to help the king. So, it is really important to me. Please help."

"Please leave," he repeated.

Quinn left and the door was locked.

The next day, they were all woken by the swaying of the ship and a strong breeze racing across its surface. Marnari was unsure what had happened. Her first reaction was that the ship had been stolen. Quinn was already up and stood at the bow of the ship. Each time the ship dipped forward, the spray covered her. She had her arms out and was laughing and screaming each time the spray hit her. Earl had not slept and he had heard the words spoken by Quinn as harsh as they were. The thing that Quinn had failed to mention to the others was that his daughter would have been about her age when she disappeared. When she had stood in front of him bawling and moaning, a part of him had seen Alara. What the others had not realised was that the captain's cabin had a secret exit that led to the hold beneath. He had emerged in the middle of the night. Unfortunately for Quinn, he had no idea that she wanted to take Clara with her so the horses had been left behind. Right now, she was having too much fun. The ship that Earl had was not one of the larger galleons or freight vessels; his was smaller, faster and lighter. Well, if you were a smuggler then you needed to be able to slip across the water as fast as you could.

He saw the others appear and greeted them.

"You have a rare one there," he said.

"Indeed, she is," said Marnari.

"I am guessing her talk got through to you," said Tullan.

"Not completely, but enough to have me think. Sorry about your horses, I didn't realise. I was told off earlier."

Tullan laughed. Having seen Quinn the day before, he too was starting to find her interesting.

"My horse can find its way home. If Clara has any sense, she will follow him. She should have the sense. They have been travelling together since I acquired her from the king's stables."

"Ha, ha," roared Earl, with laughter. "It would seem you could be just as interesting as the girl."

"Perhaps I should introduce myself then. You were out cold the first time I met you. I am Marnari Rashna."

"Aye, the girl told me. I've heard of you."

"You mean the king's mystic."

"Nope, not heard that before. You're from the order of old. Said to be the last."

"Maybe not," she said, looking at Quinn.

Quinn was now at the side of the ship; she was still laughing and squealing. Tullan couldn't understand what could be fascinating her over the side of the ship. He approached and saw a dolphin. It seemed to be chasing a ball of water. Quinn glanced up at him.

"What you doing?"

"Playing with the dolphin."

The ball would disappear and then she would twirl her hand and another one would appear, the dolphin then had to catch up to it. Tullan could hear the chatter of the dolphin each time it caught the water ball.

They had been sailing since sun up and it was now approaching mid-afternoon. The port was ahead. Quinn had stopped playing and was conversing with the dolphin. They arrived at the port and were ready to disembark. Marnari went up to Earl. "Thank you, we owe you a great debt for assisting us."

Quinn went to speak to him too.

"What will you do now? I will be disappointed if you go back to that tavern."

"No. I am done with the fishing port."

"Where then?" asked Marnari.

"East," he said. "I have to know for sure."

"You know there are no allies over there."

He roared with laughter again. "I used to be a smuggler so I know a few people on most continents. I will be fine."

Quinn was concerned by this, but was pleased that he was going to try and find his daughter.

"I don't like you being alone," said Quinn and walked to the side of the ship.

The dolphin was still there. Quinn looked across and pointed towards the stern of the ship.

"Don't leave just yet," she said, running from the ship.

Marnari and Earl were both puzzled by her request, but that was Quinn.

She came back a few moments later.

"Right, you won't be alone now," she said, once she was back.

"What do you mean? I don't need no crew."

"I doubt many would sail with you," said Marnari.

"I would," said Quinn. "Calar will travel with you. If at any time you need help, send her to me and I will find a way to help you."

Now they were even more puzzled, who was Calar? Before they could ask, she saw the look on both of their faces.

"Oh, sorry. The dolphin. I asked if she would help. She agreed."

Quinn was full of surprises. Earl looked at her.

"You better," she said and punched his gut, not that it moved.

"I will," he said.

Now they were able to depart. Quinn watched from the dock as he took his ship out again and headed east. A small figure could be seen at the side of the ship. She was glad the Calar had gone too.

Chapter 6

Having reached the northern port, they found it so dull, dark and gloomy. Very few lived there. Didn't like visitors or strangers either as they were being stared at and ignored. This was thought to be, because of the Vilhar. They had little trade, most had left for elsewhere. The band of three went to the only inn in the area. The taverns seemed to be the focal point of most towns. Nearly every traveller needs a place to stay and if you are unaccustomed to the area, then you will surely end up at the tavern for the night.

There were only two customers in the tavern and, as Marnari, Tullan and Quinn were ignored, were probably locals.

"You need a room?" came the female voice.

The owner of the establishment was a woman. Elderly and greying now. "Please," said Marnari.

The woman checked them in.

"Do you provide meals too? We have just come up by boat from the southern fishing port of Ohlan."

"I can. All of you?" she asked.

They took a seat away from the locals. It was very quiet there. Even a hushed whisper drifted around the tavern. It was hard to keep a secret here. The woman returned sometime later with the meals.

"Could I ask?" Marnari started to say.

The look from the woman was as if she already knew what she was going to say. "Do you happen to know anyone who can aid us in getting through the forest?"

"It seems to be all that anyone is interested in doing when they come here. Not that anyone who goes there comes back to tell the tale. You see the other two? The tall one, ask him."

Marnari waited until she had finished her meal and then walked the length of the tavern to the tall one.

"The innkeeper said you could possibly help me?"

"You someone looking to die then?" he said.

"Not intentionally."

"Well, there are only two reasons people come to this town. To lose themselves and forget things. Or to die, which means they are in the forest somewhere."

"Well, I don't intend to do either, but I do need to pass through the forest. There used to be a tracker who lived in this area that knew the area, but I doubt he still lives."

There was a long pause as he eyed her up and down, before he spoke.

"You've heard of Tradaris then?"

"In a manner of speaking."

She had actually met him whilst being in the service of the previous king, a long time ago. This is why she was unsure if he still lived or not.

"Head out of town, you will find three paths to the forest. Take the left path. You will find him there."

It was all he said, nothing more. He then continued to drink. She relayed the information to the others. It would seem that they should rest and then go at first light to see if they could find Tradaris. He was the best tracker and incredibly skilled, but it had been so long since he was last seen.

Marnari led the way. They had to travel on foot. The start of the forest was not too far away from the boundary of the town, only a few miles. The dark looming trees were easily seen from where they were. A single track eventually split and they did as instructed and followed the left path. This seemed to lead them away towards the ridge of the mountains. Not entirely all the way to them, but in that direction. It eventually led them to a trail into the forest. It had not been used in a long time. They stood and looked around. There was no sign of anything to indicate that anyone had a dwelling here or had even been camping here on a regular basis. The trail into the forest was overgrown and hadn't been used in a while.

"Well, I have no idea why we were led here," said Marnari.

Tullan was taking a look around to see if there were anything that they had missed.

Quinn joined him while Marnari decided what they should be doing. It was obvious that they had been misled and sent on a fool's errand.

"Marnari," said Quinn.

She was stood where the grass had become overgrown. Just peeking out the top was a wooden cross.

"I think I found him."

Marnari went to look. The cross had his name on. Why he had been buried there was unclear. Unless, it was where he fell or the local's idea of a joke. It wasn't in the forest though. She was therefore unclear why he was here. If he had fallen prey to the Vilhar, then it would have been within the confines of the forest.

"What do you want to do now?" asked Tullan.

"It would seem that we have no choice but to enter the forest on our own," responded Marnari.

"Do you happen to know where we are heading?"

"It is said to be under the mountain on the north-eastern peak." She glanced over the tree tops as she said it. There was a single peak in that direction. It was a considerable distance away. The forest extended almost the whole distance. At one point, there used to be a town that surrounded the base of the peak, but Marnari had heard about the Vilhar being more feral-like. It had been unclear why, but most chose to stay away from the area.

They cleared the path. Or Marnari did. She cast a quick spell and the brambles barring their way parted and the path was once again clear. As soon as they entered, it was like they could already feel the gaze of the forest upon them. It was good that they had started at dawn. The journey was long and they had already lost considerable time looking for someone who was no longer around. They would have to pick up the pace if they were to reach the mountain by nightfall. Even then, it was going to be a stretch.

They were going quite well. It was already noon and they had not encountered anyone. That was not what was really happening. Eyes had been upon them from the first moment they had stepped on the path. Now they were too deep into the forest to escape. The dark Vilhar, as they were otherwise known for living in the dead forest, had become tainted by the evil that had emerged here some time ago. The flora here was sickening to the Vilhar and corrupted their minds and made them turn on each other. The only way to avoid it was not to feed off the forest anymore. At one point, the Krykarins had made their way here and their vicious evil ways had been aimed to seal the fate of the Vilhar. They had intended to make them slaves to help conqueror the continent. Back then, the kingdom had been able to obtain the help from the order of mages that existed then. They had been forced to separate somet ime later. Marnari was from the order. The last of her kind. At least here, on this continent. The origins of those who had left was long since lost. It wasn't even clear if any others existed or not. This was why Marnari tried not to use her powers in the open. It would seem though that someone had taught Quinn a little magic, or as she like to call it, 'gentle' magic. Marnari had found that amusing. It was basically a non- lethal usage of the art. Having seen some of her actions and movements, it was based up on what she would call martial magic. It was an advanced combat offensive magic. That, if it was used to its full potential, was incredibly powerful. In the wrong hands, very dangerous. Whoever had taught her had not completed the training. If they had, then Quinn would realise what she had. To her, it was more like a toy that she could play with. Marnari had not been taught that way. Hers was a more practical magic. Not as lethal, but enough to most foes. She was more a scholar of magic. Not that it really bothered her.

"I think we should be able to make it before nightfall," said Tullan. Then…

That was when it happened. A cry so loud and shrill. Then another. Slowly, the cries could be heard all around the forest.

"You just had to open your mouth, didn't you," said Marnari.

Now, it was as if the forest was coming alive. They had been starting to tire, but it was always amazing how, when in a life-threatening situation, you were able to find the energy that you needed. Dark Vilhar were emerging from the trees, snarling and snapping, drool dribbling from their mouths and over their chins. Marnari could probably do something to aid them, but now they were almost on them, it would put her at risk. They were coming at them hard and fast. Quinn, even though only skilled a little, had watched Marnari earlier and seen what she did with the brambles. Her hands at each side looked like they were performing some sort of dance as they moved about. As always, regardless of who was attacking them, she didn't want to hurt them. It didn't matter that they were almost close enough to take a chunk out of her. The brambles were rising as they ran, the Vilhar were starting to get caught and some were tripping. Others, that had been paying attention, had jumped. It would seem they were very powerful. One jumped over Quinn and was clung to a tree in front of her. Before she reached him, she swept her arm right to left. The branch from the opposite tree whacked the Vilhar in the face. It was stunned by what she had done and she was easily able to slip past him on the track. Then…

Arrows went whizzing past them. Marnari looked forward. It was hard to discern those who had fired at their position, but they were not firing at them. They emerged in the clearing on the other side of the trees.

"Don't stop," came the call.

Those who stood in front of them were also Vilhar, but not tainted by the forest. They were guardians of the gateway. The last of the sane and uncorrupted Vilhar. It was thought that no more existed, but that was perhaps more to do with the fact that no one had been able to get through the forest unscathed. The dark Vilhar were falling back beyond the tree line. The chances were that they were still there and you just couldn't see them. One of the Vilhar stepped forward.

"I am Krylar, General of the Vilhar army. Well, what is left of it. We seldom get visitors, but I am sure you understand why."

"I am Marnari Rashna," she said, addressing him.

"Then I stand in esteemed company," he said.

"It would seem that you know me."

"All Vilhar know of the order of magi. Our ancestors did participate in the war of old." She knew what he meant. Even though he may not have known her personally, he had been familiar with those she was aligned with.

"Did you know a particular magus?" she asked, just out of curiosity.

"I had the good fortune to know one, as she was known then, Lady Kalakar."

Marnari was taken back. It was not that she wasn't familiar with the name, but no one had spoken that name for so long. To her, she had been so much more than just one of the order or magi. Kalakar had been her mentor.

"She doesn't use Lady anymore. A lot has changed. However, I am unclear as to her whereabouts these days, she disappeared some time ago. It is even unclear if she still lives."

"How may the Vilhar aid Marnari Rashna?"

"We wish to use the gateway."

"Then we have much to discuss. Come, you are our guests. It has been a while since anyone has been able to get this far. You are favoured, it would seem," commented Krylar.

They followed.

That night, they ate and slept well. It was too late in the day to discuss too much. General Krylar ensured his guests were well looked after. The way they were treated, one would have thought that royalty had entered the gateway city. It wasn't really known as anything else. The city surrounded the only way and means to the gateway. It was effectively a keep around the gateway. Eventually, it had just been known as the gateway city.

General Krylar was waiting in the assembly room for Marnari to join him. He had told her that he would be up at dawn as always. He was a soldier and some habits were hard to break. Even though they now only guarded the gateway and fended off the dark Vilhar, as they were commonly known to outsiders.

"I am glad you could join me," he said.

"What was so pressing that you needed to speak to me about?"

"I am afraid you have come all this way for nothing," he started to say.

"The gateway still stands?" she asked.

"Yes. It will probably stand beyond all time. That is not the problem; the city used to have two races here. The Vilhar as the protectors and the Frengris as the guardians and operators of the gate. The Frengris are no more, they have long since passed. I wish I had better news for you."

Marnari had shared a room with Quinn. It wasn't something she was usually accustomed to, but they had not been expecting guests. The shared accommodation had been the best they could do on short notice. When Marnari had risen, so had Quinn, although she didn't leave her bed until

Marnari had left and then she had sneaked out. It was still early and she was still in her nightgown. Now she was crouched hidden behind a pillar just inside the assembly hall. She wanted to know what was happening. It was her nature. Every street urchin listened to what was around them. To learn about your surroundings and others around you could have its advantages or possibly give you one. When she heard that there were no more Frengris, she knew she had to step forward.

"They haven't gone," she said.

"Quinn, this was supposed to be private," said Marnari.

"Actually, last night he considered that it would be best if you both met at dawn. It only implied he didn't specifically state it."

Krylar couldn't help but smile.

"Well, it's a good job I interpreted things my way, otherwise you would be considering to turn around. There is one who can help, but he is a long way back on our travels."

"Who?"

"Jugra'li. He is a Frengris."

Marnari had never met one so would not have been aware what he was, when she had seen him. She didn't need to ask how she knew, that part was obvious. It was clear she saw much when she looked into a person's eyes. Even the Frengris had a tale to tell.

"Where is the Frengris?" asked Krylar.

"East of the plains. He saved us from bandits," added Marnari.

"It is a long trail."

"I will have to go," said Marnari. "There is no other way."

"Then there is one who may help if you can find her."

"Who?" she asked.

"Tyca, she is said to know the whereabouts of the Tybaris."

Marnari's eyes widened at its mention.

"It cannot be; that it is nothing more than a fable told throughout the cities by travellers," said Marnari.

Tybaris was said to have been created during the great war and lost.

"I have heard it too in the capital. Many of us would gather 'round to listen. It is a beast of great power and speed. It can kill with a single strike and run faster than the wind. The beast can never be caught or killed," said Quinn.

"Well, regardless of fabled tales. Tyca is said to know where to find the beast."

"Where is Tyca?" asked Quinn.

"The area at the north-western part of the forest."

"Then I shall have to be careful," said Marnari. "Where are you going?"

Quinn had turned to leave.

"To wash and get dressed," she said, smiling, "it will be breakfast soon."

Marnari nodded, she needed to prepare.

Chapter 7

Quinn splashed the water across her face that was in the bowl and quickly changed. Now she made her way to the kitchens.

"Excuse me," she said. "Is there a chance of an early breakfast, preferably to take with me. Lady Marnari has me running errands."

The head cook gave her some freshly cooked bread and ham then she was off. If you wanted someone to believe in what you were saying, then you had to believe in it yourself.

"Where do you think you are going at this time of day?" said the guard at the main gate to the city.

"Errands," she said, looking straight at the guard.

"Who would be stupid enough to send a young girl out through the main gates to run errands?"

"My mentor," she started to say, "Lady Marnari from the order of the magi. She believes a few ingredients from the forest should be enough to aid us in our travels."

"I don't think I should let you out."

"That's fine, I didn't want to go anyway, but you will have to answer to Lady Marnari when she finds out. Perhaps you will be guarding the gates on the outside tomorrow," she said, walking away.

Quinn had been casually snacking as she spoke. The ham was still warm and had a strong scent, it was even making the guard hungry.

"Be quick," he said, letting her pass.

The cleared area to the forest was safe, but Quinn had no intention of letting anyone know what her real intentions were. She said thank you and handed the guard the last of her ham. The bread would do for later, well, what was left of it. She shoved it into her pack and set off. There was no time to waste. Being alone, she might be able to elude the dark Vilhar. Once she entered into the forest, she picked up the pace. Her hands were ready if she needed to use any evasive magic. Quinn knew that she would not be able to defeat a beast in an open fight. She hadn't got it in her to kill someone. She moved as quickly as she could, which was a reasonable pace.

Living on the streets, she had to be able to avoid the guards. Not that she would deliberately do anything to annoy them, but one urchin looked like another on the streets so it was easy to mistake one for another in a chase. After a time, if you saw a guard chasing someone, then you just ran. It was safer. Quinn thought she was doing well. Then, as always, the trees and the bushes started to rustle. It did her no good to look or even watch. She was better off not knowing how many were chasing her.

"You all set?" said Tullan. "Are you sure I can't go in your stead?"

"No, I will be fine. Just keep an eye on Quinn."

Tullan nodded as they approached the gates. The guard looked at Lady Marnari as she had been named earlier that day. He had been thankful for the remainder of the ham.

"Can you let me leave?" she said. "I will be gone a while."

"Off to fetch your apprentice?" he said. "She late back from her errands?"

"Excuse me?" she asked.

"Your apprentice, she was most insistent about leaving. Said you had given her errands."

"Oh, Quinn, what are you doing?" she said. "Where is General Krylar at this hour?"

"He will be making his rounds."

Marnari walked off to look for the General to inform him that Quinn had deceived them all.

"You're not going after her?" enquired Tullan.

"Wouldn't know where to start. I just hope she knows what she is doing."

"Do you even know why?"

"Yes. She spoke with the Frengris so feels responsible and he may not speak to me as he only spoke to her. Damn that girl."

Quinn was still running. The forest was vast and she had no idea how much longer she had to keep running at this pace, but she suspected that if she faltered, they would strike. As long as she seemed strong, then she would be safe, but she had not run this fast for so long before. Her legs were aching bad. There was no choice, she had to try and hope she was close enough.

"Tyca," she called.

Her legs would buckle under her if she was not careful.

"TYCA!" she screamed.

Then she slipped on a wet root. Her legs had been too tired to step over. Stumbling forward, she immediately dived into a forward roll and was back on her feet. That one slip-up had been enough, now they had emerged from the trees. They ran, one on each side of her. She had no other choice. It was them or her. Remembering what had happened at Broson's place and what Marnari had said, she tried it.

"Vreshna," and threw her arms to the side. The dark Vilhar smashed into the trees on their flanks. Now they were dazed. To kill them would have required a more powerful throw. More were appearing behind. She shouldn't have done this, it was wrong. Quinn knew that she was not strong enough, she tried again.

"TYCA, PLEASE."

She was almost begging. Then she fell. Her legs had gone. She didn't even have the strength to roll. Now on her rear and hands behind, she was trying to scramble away. The Vilhar had slowed and were cautiously approaching. Snarling and growling at her, they had seen what she could do. One fell as an arrow went clean through its side and hit a second, the beasts turned only to be felled. Quinn looked towards the mountains. Her aim had been off; she had run to the range, not the north-west. More arrows were released and more fell. A young-looking, raven-haired woman jumped from the rock she was stood on. It was tied back as it was so long. As both feet hit the ground, another arrow was released. With each shot, she had been getting closer to Quinn. She smelled the air and reached into Quinn's pack.

"Hey," Quinn said as she took her bread.

Tyca didn't eat it. She ripped it into several pieces and threw it through the air in the direction of the Vilhar.

"Better they eat that than you. So, who are you?"

"I'm guessing you're Tyca, thank you. I'm Apprentice Quinn."

"A magic caster, go home," she said and walked away.

"I need your help to find the Tybaris."

She stopped in her tracks. It had been a long time since anyone had come to enquire about Tybaris.

"Why?"

"I have to find the last Frengris and so I need the Tybaris for its speed."

"Go home, the Frengris are all dead."

"No. One lives, Jugra'li."

Tyca stopped and looked back. She couldn't just leave the girl. It wasn't her fault she was aligned with the magi.

"Come, we need to get to high ground. The Restar can't climb."

"Restar?"

"Those who were chasing you. Outsiders call them dark Vilhar. Those at the city named them Restar, it means the rest of us. If you wish to live, move."

They reached the mountain range.

"Right, you go that way."

"Why?"

Tyca had pointed south on the range, not north.

"I understand the Tybaris is north and you know the way," said Quinn.

"I don't have anything to do with the magi anymore. Please leave."

Quinn was able to catch a quick glimpse in her eyes.

"What happened? Was she a friend, a sister, a relative?"

Tyca kept walking and so did Quinn, north. She knew that she had followed. Quinn was not the quietest on the rocks.

"Make less noise. You couldn't creep up on anyone," said Tyca, after they had been walking a while. "Anyone ever tell you that you're stubborn?"

"Yes, many times. Even Marnari Rashna."

Tyca stopped and turned, "You're travelling with her?"

"I'm her apprentice."

"Why?"

"I see things, which is how I know about you. Who was she?"

"Who?"

"The one who died."

Tyca stopped and sat down. It had been a long time since she had spoken about her, although she was always in her thoughts.

"My best friend, Talia. She was the daughter of a magus. The one they called Lady Kalakar. She died though and I lost my best friend. Her mother disappeared and no one has seen her since."

"The General mentioned her name. How did your friend die?"

"Giving birth."

"What happened to the child?"

"I presume dead too, never heard of one surviving the birth."

"I'm sorry, but I so need your help."

"Why?" it was Tyca's turn to ask the questions.

"The king is dead and General Crellis is the only one who may know of an heir."

"I see, but there is no heir."

"How come you are so certain?" asked Quinn.

"Because I am."

"Will you tell me how to find Tybaris? Please."

"There is a full moon tonight. If you are to find it, then it will appear in the open glade north of here. The moon will light the whole area."

"How do I get it to come?"

"I have no idea. I can only take you there, but I cannot stay. Remember the beast maybe fast, but it is also a killer. Don't ever forget that."

"I won't. Thank you."

"For what?"

"Helping," replied Quinn.

"How do you know that you won't die when you meet it?"

"I won't."

Tyca looked at her. Quinn seemed so sure of herself.

It was approaching midnight and the moon was high. There were no clouds in sight. Tyca had left, she could not stay. It was not her place. Quinn was alone. She stood in the centre of the glade. She had no idea what type of beast this was. No one had said during the conversation earlier that day. Quinn was unsure what to do, so she did what she usually did.

"Tybaris," she called. "If you are there, I need your help. The king has been slain and I need to find the last Frengris to pass through the gateway. It is the way I have chosen."

Initially, it had been to take Clara with her, but she had been left at the fishing port by Earl. Not that he knew. To a degree, it didn't really matter about passing through the gate. They could have just gone north to Uboria with Tullan and caught a ship there, but they still felt compelled to pass through the gateway. They had almost achieved that goal too.

A howl was heard, echoing through the forest. Its cry was even loud enough to reach those at the gateway. Marnari was on the ramparts. She heard the cry and knew Quinn was safe. The beast would not have cried out, if she had not called for it.

"Now, we wait," said Marnari.

What appeared, as Quinn stood there, was not what she had expected. The largest wolf beast she had ever seen emerged from the trees on the northern side. It was unlike anything she had ever seen before. It was even larger than Marnari's horse. The wolf was completely black, head to toe. The only distinguishing feature was its red eyes. It stepped forward and circled the perimeter of the glade. All the time it walked, the beast had its eyes on Quinn. She was unsure what to do next. Then it was back in front of her, it approached. Then, something totally unexpected happened. It even surprised Quinn when it happened.

"Why should I trust you?" said Tybaris.

"You shouldn't," said Quinn, after a moment's pause to comprehend a talking beast and realising it was female.

"Then leave."

"I was the one who spoke with the Frengris. I saw in his eyes like I can see in yours. No one has needed you for a long time. That is why you came tonight. You are tied to this place."

"You read souls," said the beast.

Was the beast old and ancient, had it seen many things in its life? Quinn wasn't sure. To some it was a creation, someone who had the chance and opportunity to understand things from another life. At least in some tales told.

There had not been anyone who could read a soul in a long time. If she remembered correctly, it was many hundreds of years past.

"I guess that is one way of putting it. Marnari and I need to find someone who may know the existence of an heir."

"What if one does not exist?"

"I have to help. Marnari is the first in a long time to take an interest in me. I am sure from what I saw about you that you can relate to that. Please help me do this?"

The beast had been circling her as it listened.

"Very well," she said, lowering her front leg so that Quinn could climb onto her back. "You better hold on tight."

Chapter 8

The beast was moving through the forest as fast as it was able. It could not move that fast yet as the trees did not give a clear path. Tybaris was indeed bound to the forest as when it had cried out, the Restar had all heard. Now, they had only one task. Stop the Tybaris. The beast had not been called in so long and if it had, it never emerged. This night, it chose to appear and listen to what Quinn had to say. Now it had agreed to help. This meant that its bond would be broken with the forest, but it also meant so much more too.

As they left the forest, so did the Restar. They had to hunt and kill the Tybaris. The Tybaris had been created long ago. It was only meant to be a temporary measure, but something was wrong. Tyca had grown to hate the magi. It was because of them that the Tybaris had been created and bound to the forest. The beast was never meant to be bound and was meant to eradicate the dark Vilhar, who became the Restar. They were a newly appointed magus and even though they had good intentions, they were overzealous and screwed the process up. With it, a life was lost. Now the beast had become cursed to roam the forest, but if it ever chose to leave, then it should have a reason beyond anything. Once it chose to leave, the dark Vilhar would be freed of their attachment to the forest and would be able to leave. Their sole purpose was to kill the Tybaris. Now they hunted it. The bond was fragile; it had to return to the grove within twenty-four hours if it was to live. Even though the bond was broken, hope still remained. Some considered hope to be an empty four-lettered word, as more often than not, hope came with disappointment.

"No matter what, do not loosen your grip," said Tybaris.

It was free from the forest. Now it howled to the world. Tybaris had been lost and hidden for so long. Now, she was back and had decided, because of this one girl's courage, to seek her out, to take up the mantle again. It would come with a high cost, especially if the Restar caught her. Her true purpose had been that of a protector. The great war needed that extra edge, but ultimately, they lost to the Krykarins. The most they succeeded in doing was forcing them off their land and back to theirs, but that had never meant the threat was over. There would be many Krykarins who would love to end the life of the beast that had taken so many of them in the war. So, by reappearing, she had two enemies. Once she was dead, the Restar could no longer be contained in the forest.

Her speed was no match for the Restar that had followed. They were hot on their trail and had no intention of stopping. They had a chance now that the beast was back. While the two were still bound, the general populace were not at risk, unless you were aiding the Tybaris, which Quinn would be considered doing. She had called it forth and it had responded to her and now the two were connected. Quinn had no idea what she had done. Marnari had more understanding. She was worried for Quinn, because she knew exactly what it meant when the beast had cried out.

She knew how the beast had been created, even though she wasn't present at the mess that had been made. It should never had been allowed, but times had become desperate. It had made her ashamed to be a magus. What they had done and unleashed! Neberin had died during that war and his mess still lived, cursed to walk the land for all time. He would have been the only one to have given information as to what he did wrong in his casting, but he had been killed before anyone could question him.

Her speed was incredible. Quinn found it hard to breathe as the air felt like it was being forced away from her face as they moved. She had to lean forward; her head was almost lying on the back of Tybaris' neck. The beast could not hang around and so long as Quinn was on her back, could not defend or attack. Her leaps and bounds covered great distances. Brooks were crossed in a single leap and the fields she covered so quickly. Only trees slowed her down. She had to twist and turn. Some areas were unavoidable. They knew roughly where to go. It wasn't long before she was racing down the edge of the hot dusty plains. Her speed eased.

"Quinn. Do you remember where?"

She lifted her head. What she could remember was vague, it had been her first time out of the city and there had been too much to see and take in. They were reaching the edge of the plains.

"Turn east," she called.

They reached the meadow she had been in before when she had met the Frengris.

"Jugra'li," called Quinn.

She kept repeating the cry, but now they were stood still. They had been able to get ahead of the Restar. It wouldn't be long before they found them again.

"Dismount," said Tybaris.

She was able to smell the Restar, they were near. They had stopped in one place too long.

"Take cover in the trees," she said to Quinn.

"Why?" she asked.

An answer was not necessary as she saw several packs running from the top end of the meadow.

"Run."

Quinn didn't hesitate, but she feared for the Tybaris. She was surrounded. Tybaris leapt forwards, her jaw wide. Her jaw was able to take a whole head and crush it with her teeth. Several fell, the Restar started to get more organised. She was now slowly being pushed back. It would be night fall soon and she would need to get back to the dead forest. She knew what they intended to do. If they could keep her away for too long, then they would be free and she would be easier to kill. More would be able to leave and find her. Once she was dead, they would have no means to control the Restar.

Quinn was watching from the trees as she was not there with Tybaris. Right now, she was not in any immediate danger, but if they were to kill the Tybaris right now, then they would be able to smell its scent on her and then she would be hunted too. The Restar were lashing out. There were too many. She was able to get one or two more. The consequences of her actions were telling on her. Quinn had no way to help. Tears started to run down her face. The Tybaris was hurt on one leg. Soon, she would not be able to run back to the forest.

"JUGRA'LI," she screamed, in desperation.

He had heard, but had been too far away. Jugra'li had recognised the voice of the one who had been kind. What he hadn't expected was to hear or see her again. That was the way of most he encountered. They were afraid of the gentle giant, but Quinn wasn't. The gift she had allowed her to see deep into his soul. It had only been a moment, but it was enough to know who he was and that he considered himself to be the last of his kind. They were now jumping on Tybaris's back, the added weight and the pain in her leg made it hard to lash back at them. It wouldn't be long before they had her on the ground. Then…

Whack!

Jugra'li saw why he had been called. He knew what they were and why they were here. Considering he was Frengris, he had once lived in the forest, before it had been dark and had learned about the creation of the beast Tybaris. The Restar's head was crushed as he hit it hard. While he dealt with those on the ground, Tybaris was able to reach around and pull the others from her back. It wasn't long before the two of them had eliminated the Restar, but that was only the first wave.

Quinn ran forward. She hugged the Frengris as soon as she reached. "Thank you for coming."

"It isn't over yet," said Tybaris.

She had spied more on approach.

"Jugra'li, how far can you throw your staff?" asked Quinn.

He grunted and shrugged his shoulders. It was something he had never been asked before. He spoke very little. There was never anyone around to share a conversation with.

"Aim for the Restar," she said. "I will do the rest."

What she was about to attempt had never been tried by her before, certainly not with something so large. A ball in the city streets was easy, but this was new. She stood in front of Tybaris and grounded her feet, firm and hard against the surface of the meadow. Now her upper body started to rotate, a breeze was forming around them. As Quinn swayed so did the grass surrounding them.

"Get ready," she instructed.

Still swaying, more and more. Preparing for what was to happen next. "NOW!"

Jugra'li released the staff. As soon as it left his hands Quinn caught it in the breeze she had created. There had been a lot of preparation. She had never put that much effort into her gentle magic before. As the staff end approached the one on the right, she swayed her body and arms in one motion in an anticlockwise direction. The staff arced across the meadow and slammed into the charging Restar, because of its size they were unable to avoid the striking staff. Each had been rendered unconscious. Quinn was no longer able to maintain the breeze and the staff dropped to the ground, as did she. She had passed out from the effort.

Tybaris could not smell anymore Restar. They had time to act. Her leg had stopped bleeding. She would have no real speed now. So, if more came, she would be vulnerable.

"Put her on my back, we have to leave."

"Leave," said Jugra'li.

"She came to ask for your help. You are the only one who can."

He looked at her puzzled.

"She needs to use the gateway. The king is dead. It is believing an heir exists, but I have never known of this. You are the only one who can open it for her. She has risked everything to find you. Will you aid her?" she asked.

Jugra'li had some rope and was securing Quinn to the back of Tybaris.

"I…" he started to say, then looked at Quinn. The one who had chosen him as a friend. "Yes."

"Then we don't have much time. I have none as I need to return. If I don't leave now, the Restar will be free before I return."

Jugra'li nodded, he understood only too well what that meant. He lumbered up the meadow to collect his staff. Tybaris had already left. She couldn't wait any longer.

The sun was almost at rest. There was little time left. Tybaris was not going to make it.

"I have failed," she said.

Quinn had regained consciousness some time ago and hadn't wanted to distract her. She lifted her head and looked out to the west. The sun was almost gone, but the forest was in sight. She lay back down on Tybaris and hugged her real tight. "I believe in you," she said, "you can make it."

Tybaris suddenly felt a warmth fill her. It was as if Quinn was lending her energy to complete her task. She felt renewed and full of life. Her speed was increasing. Each leap and bound was as it had been when they first left. The sun dipped out of sight. She had already cleared the trees and howled. Tybaris howled so loud and so long. Her intention was to let every single Restar know that they had failed. It did more than that though. Those at the city were aware of their return. Marnari smiled. They were back, but had they been able to find the Frengris?

Tybaris needed to return to the glade, she didn't slow her speed, but used the last of what Quinn had provided her to complete her journey. Reaching under, she snapped the rope that bound Quinn to her. She was then able to climb down to the ground. "Come with me," said Tybaris.

The two of them walked through the trees from where she had originally emerged. Now she led Quinn to the place where she would rest and sleep until called again. This was her home. Her home was nothing more than a grove of tightly grown group of trees. The canopy protected her form the sky and the trunks from the elements. She was safe here. I had been made a safe place for her as was the glade. Anywhere else in the dead forest could mean her death. It had been all the magi could do considering the curse she bore. In the back of her den was a box. It was old, scuffed and damaged.

"Open it," she said to Quinn.

Inside was a necklace.

"Take it and give it to Tyca and tell her thank you for protecting me all these years, but now I ask her to aid and protect you."

Quinn looked at her, unsure why she would need Tyca to protect her.

"One last thing. Tell her I have missed her so much."

Then she lay down and closed her eyes. Quinn left to find Tyca and return to the City. Jugra'li would be there soon.

Chapter 9

Jugra'li arrived the next day, it had been quite a trek for him. He had not been here in a very long time. The forest still looked very foreboding, the darkness that existed there seemed to consume everything that it touched or those who went near it. When the Vilhar had become tainted by the forest, it was the day he left. It was not a good sign and he didn't like what he saw. The Frengris had always lived beneath the mountain. The Vilhar became the protectors of the gateway. Back then the Frengris were peaceful, but soon learned. The great war changed many things, including the Frengris. The Vilhar suffered. The forest became cursed and those who fed from the plants grown in its soil were tainted and eventually became the Restar.

He stood for a moment. Being here again was not what he had wanted or even planned for, but the young girl had asked for his help. She was the first to be kind to him in a very long time. It was for her that he had returned. The Frengris had a few rituals of their own. He was home and the mountain had to be told of his arrival. This was no small task. Now he took his staff, part way up, between his two strong hands and started to pound the end that was in contact with the ground slowly. It built up until he had a rhythm. Now he increased the pounds and speed. The ground was starting to shake. The Restar were awake. They knew what it meant. Jugra'li continued this for almost an hour. Relentless with his actions, not faulting once, because of his incredible strength and stamina. The vibrations were strong enough to reach even the city walls. General Krylar went to the wall of the city and climbed to the rampart wall and looked out over the forest. Quinn had been waiting a long time for Jugra'li.

"What is that noise?" she asked.

He looked down and smiled at her.

"Your friend is home. He is welcoming the mountain. Now we wait. TO ARMS," he called.

The Restar would be awake and aware. As soon as the Frengris entered the forest, they would hunt him.

Tyca had been found the day before; she was on the rocks as she was each day. Her vigil to watch over the glade. Quinn was aware of much more since she had last seen her. As Tybaris had spoken to her, she had looked deep into her eyes and knew everything. How, why and when the Tybaris had come to be! She also knew the connection to Tybaris and Tyca and understood the importance of the necklace.

"Thank you," she said.

"You are welcome."

"You knew she would come, didn't you?" asked Quinn.

"I wasn't completely sure, it has been a while."

"She is home now and safe," she continued. "Before I left her though, she asked me to seek you out."

Tyca sat down on the rock to listen. She had not seen or spoken to Tybaris in a long time. Then Quinn extended her hand and opened it. On her palm lay the necklace. A tear started to form at the corner of Tyca's eye. She had not seen that in a long time. "Told me to say thank you for protecting her."

Tyca took the necklace and placed it around her neck. It was back with her now. The necklace had been a gift, but she had left it with Tybaris. Now it was returned, it meant only one thing.

"She said something else, didn't she? Otherwise, I wouldn't have the necklace back."

"Tybaris asked for you to protect me."

"Then I will."

"I know who she is and what she means to you," said Quinn. "If you want to stay, I won't stop you."

"No. She has asked and I need to honour that and please keep what you know to yourself. It could only endanger her and me."

Quinn nodded. Tyca picked up her bow and the two headed towards the city. That had been yesterday.

Tyca came up the ramparts to speak with the General, she also knew what was happening. Jugra'li had announced himself to the mountain, but much more too. "General," she said, addressing him. "I need to leave."

"I can't let you risk your life."

"If you know anything about me, you will realise that I can just as easily grab a rope and climb out. I considered it polite to ask first."

Quinn turned and looked at her. Tyca could see the concern in his eyes.

"He will need help. The General cannot commit his men, but I am not one of them. With your permission, Miss Quinn."

Since she had agreed to protect her then she had been given that title now, by Tyca. Marnari had not understood why she had been elected to be Quinn's protector, but there was nothing she could do about it. Things were changing, in many ways. Quinn could only nod. It was all so strange to her. She had been a street urchin, then an apprentice, now she was Miss Quinn. The General barked his orders to the guards below.

Tyca slipped out. Her bow was in her hand. She was ready, but first, she had to let the Restar know that she would be hunting them. At her side was a horn. Taking hold of it, she placed it against her lips, then with one long blast, blew into it.

Wherever the Restar were, they stopped and listened. It wasn't the first time they had heard that noise. Their prime concern was the Frengris. It had announced itself.

They would need to kill it first. Their numbers were vast. Some were definitely going to die today. Once she had finished, she was off. Not a fast pace, but a steady trot. An arrow was already notched. As soon as she approached the trees, she fired. Then raised the horn and gave two sharp blasts then she was gone.

"Why did she do that?" asked Quinn.

"First blood. To let them know that one of theirs just died," said the General.

"Has she done this before?"

"Many times. Each time she has heard of a fallen traveller, she will hunt and take ten Restar for each victim."

"And they have never caught her?"

"No. I guess she is just that good," replied General Krylar.

"If she is no longer able to protect the Tybaris, what will happen to her?"

"Was she awake when you left?"

"No. Sleeping," replied Quinn, a little unsure about why.

"Then she is safe. It was the only way the magi could give protection for the mess that had been caused. So it's told, I wasn't there then."

Tyca moved quietly and slowly. She would not use the horn again. The first two were enough, they knew to be wary. Many, over the years, had already fallen to her. Another Restar dropped, it had been skulking in the bushes. Soon she would meet up with Jugra'li. He had entered the forest too. The horn was something he was not familiar with. It was very awkward to wield his staff in the forest like he could in the open.

Considering the space between the trees, he would have been wise to leave the staff behind, but it had been with him for a very long time. It would be a shame to lose it. The paths used to be wider in the past. Now they were overgrown and so the way was hard. It was also difficult to remember the correct route. The horn had helped with that. Now he had a direction to move in.

Slam, smash, crack!

Skulls were being smacked. The Restar were not easy to attack in the trees either. This was why they chased until you were tired. Jugra'li would not tire. The way ahead was starting to clear, there was a brief open area. Now he increased his speed to reach it. The Restar had been waiting. They had calculated where he would be and attacked, but Jugra'li was now able to swing the staff he had in his hand. He swung it in a wide arc, splitting skulls like they were rotten apples. As fast as he cleared them, more appeared. It wasn't a problem as he just opened up even more, but they were preventing him from passing.

One howled to let the others know where he was. Tyca heard it too and knew what was going to happen. They intended to surround him. A Frengris may be large and tough, but he was alone. This is what she had feared. It was the same tactic they had adopted to try and kill Tybaris. She hadn't got time for the bow and slung it over her body and drew two daggers. There was no time to waste. She encountered the dark form of a Restar. They were not unlike the Vilhar, but had a darkness about them. The skin had become almost black and they had become wilder, almost feral. She drew a blade across its throat and kept moving. Each one she met died. They were easy enough to kill, if alone, but tended to hunt in packs. This is why Jugra'li was about to have a major problem.

Packs had been grouping together, ready and waiting to strike. Jugra'li had not realised just how many were lurking in the shadows of the trees. Tybaris had a protector; he had his staff. He swung in a three hundred and sixty rotation, pivoting on his feet. All Restar that were close to him fell. Now they appeared. Packs of Restar emerged, slow and calculating, they advanced on him. He had not expected too many to appear. The numbers were overwhelming. He may be strong, but that only carried him so far. Their snarling, growling faces watched him. Jugra'li prepared, then they charged. He swung again, taking what he could, before they all took hold of his staff. It was immovable now. They had managed to disarm him. He would not be able to recover it at this time. All he had now was his two strong hands. One jumped at him he grabbed its head and ripped the jaw apart. Then another charged, followed by more. He was now only able to punch them; it was not easy to stop them. They were forcing him back, but he had not realised that they were behind him too. Not until he could feel their breath on his back. He was taller than them and looked around to see just how many were attacking. Now he kicked out and thumped downwards onto the top of their heads. He was completely penned in. There was nowhere to go. Their claws drawn, the Restar started to slash at his legs and torso. Jugra'li cried out. Tyca had heard his cry and knew he was in trouble. She had no choice and gave three blasts on the horn. She needed them to know she was there and more importantly for Jugra'li to know she was close and not to give up. He was now down on his knees, they had been cut really badly. It was not possible to stand right now. As soon as he fell, they were on him. No matter how close she was, it might not make a difference.

Tyca had taken to the trees. She was very agile and nimble. Now she was perched at the edge of the clearing and fired. The arrow speared many as it went through them. Then she fired again. She was on Jugra'li's right and kept firing in one concentrated area. Tyca didn't have enough arrows to deal with all of the enemy, but she could take the pressure off him at one point.

"Jugra'li," she called, so he knew she was there.

Arrows kept raining into the Restar. She didn't stop, too much was at stake. If he died, then they would never open the gateway. Also, Jugra'li was a friend of Miss Quinn. That was important to her, so that meant he had to survive. Slowly one side was being cleared.

"Run, to the trees," she called.

He didn't need to be told twice. Moving towards her, he slipped into the shadows. Tyca stayed where she was. Her quiver was almost empty, but she had no intention of moving yet. Now she was down to her last few arrows. Time to go. In a skittish manner, she moved back through the trees along the branches. Jugra'li' was not doing well. She had only one hope left to get them to safety. They needed help. Let's just hope he remembered. She gave two sharp blasts on the horn, followed by one long dull tone. Tyca had not called him in a long time. He lived high on the mountain. She so hoped that he was still alive. It had been so long since her friend had been with her, but for his own safety she had dismissed to protect him. A cry came from above. He lived. She was so glad. They heard too at the city.

"It can't be," said Marnari.

She had known about such a hawk, but this too she had believed to be a fabled creature. It was what was called a shadow hawk. The bird was completely black, head to talon, even its eyes were too. It had been bitten by an evil beast created by the makings of the Krykarins. Back before the war. Then, that would mean that Tyca was… No, it couldn't be! All this time and she still lived. Back in the war, she was known as the shadow huntress and had lost a dear younger sister during the war. Now she knew why she was here. To protect! Quinn was in very safe hands. Things were definitely being stirred up. Yet, none of this would have happened if they had caught a ship out of Uboria. She glanced over at Quinn. Who was she? Had she known?

Too much was changing too fast. The Frengris, Tybaris and now the shadow huntress and her hawk.

The beast was four times larger than any other hawk. It was very fast too. Tyca had befriended the beast. When it had been bitten, she had cared and tended to its needs, after she had stolen it from the Krykarins. The biting was part of the ritual to change and taint the newborn creature. The hawk had then become loyal to her. For a while, it had helped her protect

Tybaris, but then the Restar had grown in numbers and she feared for its life and sent it away. It had never gone far; finding refuge in the high peaks of the mountain, it had stayed close by. It swooped down, its talons drawn, and grabbed a running Restar and then went after another. The hawk cried out as it saw Tyca. It was pleased she had finally called to him. It had been many years since he had last seen her.

General Krylar had seen where the hawk had dived and called to the garrison. Those on the walls prepared for the Restar. He left the ramparts and joined his men below. The gates were opened and they exited. If she had called the hawk after all this time, then things really were bad. He knew he had no choice, but to go and aid them. Even though he knew every Vilhar would stand behind him, the city could not be left unguarded. So, with a dozen hardened soldiers, they ran towards the trees. The Restar were there, waiting. What they had not expected was the Vilhar to attack. That never happened. None had entered the darkness of the forest, ever. They started to carve a path towards Tyca and Jugra'li.

It wasn't long before they found them both. Tyca dropped from the trees when she saw the General.

"Thanks."

Her and Jugra'li entered the clearing and the gates were reopened. The Vilhar started to fall back. They had succeeded and were safe for now. The Restar would lick their wounds and would be back in the shadows, waiting for their next victim.

Chapter 10

Quinn greeted both of them with a hug. She saw how badly Jugra'li had been injured.

"He has been poisoned," said Tyca, seeing the leg wounds. "There is no way to extract it."

Quinn didn't hesitate. "Tullan, a full bucket of water, quickly please."

Even Marnari had no idea what she wanted it for. The water would not wash away the poison. Tullan returned. Quinn had crouched next to where Jugra'li had lain on the floor.

"I need a minute," said Quinn, "when I say throw the water over his legs, do it."

Her hands were moving in the air and she was mumbling something very quietly to herself. Even with Marnari straining her ears, she was unable to hear what was being said.

"Now."

Tullan did as asked. Quinn had her hands ready. She had only ever been shown this; she had never actually performed it. Her mumblings were recalling what had been said to her about the method to do this. As the water covered his legs, she caught it with her hands over his legs. Once she had all of it, her right hand held it there. The left hand had to perform the necessary task. That was a very important part of the procedure. Her emotions were part of the process and they came best from the left side. The side closest to the heart. Her feelings for her friends were strong. Until she had left the city, friends had not been a part of her life, now she had several. Her left hand was moving the water around his legs. Some of the poison on the surface of his leg was being diluted. That would not be enough.

"Hold him," said Quinn, "tightly."

No one moved unsure why as he was not in any distress. Quinn's hand was open with her fingers extended to the max. Now she slowly moved her fingers in towards her palm. The water started to constrict around his leg and was squeezing on the wounds. The poison was starting to be forced out. Marnari had never seen magic like this before and by the method used, knew that Quinn could not have come up with this on her own.

"It's not enough," said Tyca.

Quinn raised her head and looked at Jugra'li, "I'm sorry."

"You tried your best," he said.

"That's not what I meant."

She slammed her fingers into the palm of her hand and Jugra'li screamed out. Now they realised why he had to be held. The General grabbed one arm and Tyca the other. He was a strong person and it was hard to hold him down. Tullan and Marnari had to go and assist them both. The water around Jugra'li's legs was black from the poison. She needed more clean water.

"Guard," Quinn called, to the nearest person. "I need clean water."

He looked across at the General who nodded. The water was fetched quickly. Quinn was unable to move whilst she did this. She dropped her right hand, which instantly allowed the water on Jugra'li to hit the ground. The guard threw the fresh clean water over him.

"Be ready with more if I need it."

She repeated the process. The pain was less for him now as the majority of the poison had already been forced from his body. The water was only half saturated this time. She dropped it to the floor again and the guard covered Jugra'li one last time. Quinn sat quietly as she held the water around his legs. Jugra'li was breathing easier now. The threat was gone, but Quinn stayed sat at his side with the water around his wounds. The water was soothing and helped to ease any remaining pain. Later when she had finished, Tyca picked her up and carried her to a bed to sleep and rest, she was exhausted. Jugra'li was able to get up and walking was easier. He too needed rest.

Marnari took the period of rest to seek out Tyca. She was on the ramparts. Her gaze was fixed on the north-west.

"You're the shadow huntress," she said, standing next to her.

"What gave it away?" Tyca replied.

"The hawk. Only one person has ever been seen with a black hawk."

"Then I guess you have lived as long as I have."

"I was a lot younger during the great war so I had only seen a little of the magi at that time and still had much to learn."

"So, you were an apprentice during that time. Who was your mentor?"

"Kalakar."

Tyca was now the one to be surprised. Magus Kalakar rarely took a student. She was impressed. It also made her realise who Marnari was.

"You're the last of the magi in this realm. Or as the old king called you, the mystic."

"Nothing mystical about me, but he used to like to have fun with his advisors."

"What brought you here?"

"Well, Quinn, but we had a task to perform. The king has been killed, Lord Broson had him assassinated. Quinn and I were at Lord Broson's when it happened. We were lucky to get out. If it wasn't for Quinn's gift, we may be dead and not here."

"Gift?"

"She can read souls."

"Oh."

Tyca now realised that she would know then. The secret that she had kept to herself all these years. Perhaps Tybaris also knew about Quinn and that is why she had been told to protect her. The huntress would not fail. She aligned herself to no one. Only those that she chose, but this had been chosen for her. That didn't matter considering who had chosen for her. Now she had a better understanding. She readily accepted the task now. It was now getting late. Hopefully, they could move forward. Until they found Crellis, they had no idea what would be in store for finding the heir if indeed it was true.

Quinn was up at dawn, her bright and cheerful self, as always. The first thing she did was visit the kitchen, not just for her. She gathered up extra and went to enquire where Jugra'li was. Her arms were laden with so much food as she sat on the edge of his bed.

“I am glad you survived,” she said.

“I came because you asked.”

“That isn’t why I am glad. It is because you are my friend.”

Now she laid the food down.

“You need to eat to get your strength up. I am not sure what you need to do with the gateway, but regardless, you will need to be able to walk there.”

Tyca found the two of them later. She had been to check on her and saw that she was gone and immediately became worried. One of the guards told here where she had gone, so she just followed her tracks.

“Apple,” said Quinn, throwing one to her.

“You bounced back quickly.”

“I guess living on the streets has made me that way. You never know from day to day what will happen, so you have to be up at dawn and ready for anything. The first thing you always start with is what will your meal be for the day.”

It was around noon that Jugra’li felt strong enough to walk. He had a task to perform for Quinn. Tullan had been talking to Marnari overnight. He had come this far and if they were willing, he would like to continue the journey with them; it was becoming quite the adventure. Marnari had stressed that with everything she had witnessed, the trail ahead would only get more treacherous. He understood. Tyca held back as they made their way towards the gate.

“I need a moment, I will catch up.”

Quinn saw in her eyes the concern she had.

“That is fine,” she said and smiled.

They proceeded to the gate. This was not the gateway. All this did was bar the way to the tunnels that led beneath the mountain. The gateway was further inside. Quinn stared at the door. There were two holes, high up in the shape of hands with fingers spread. She could see now why a Frengris was needed. Jugra'li reached up and put his hands inside where there were two discs. Now he pushed and twisted the two discs outward and away from each other. There was a click as they reached the point he moved them to. Now, he retracted his hands and pushed on the gates. That was just the means to gain entry to the tunnel. Now they had a walk down to the gateway. The slope that was the trail down had not been used in a long time. The air that escaped was stale. They waited a moment for a balancing breeze to blow inwards. Jugra'li led the way.

Tyca blew on her horn to summon the hawk. It appeared and sat on the ground. Sitting in front of her, it was almost as tall as Quinn. The bird seemed to understand everything she said and likewise, she understood his cries.

"Hello, old friend," she said giving the bird a hug. "I would like to ask a favour of you." He cried in response.

"I have to travel to the north. Tybaris asks that I protect the one called Miss Quinn. I fear for Tybaris and ask that you take my place and guard her until I am able to return."

The hawk cried out twice.

"Thank you."

Then he took to the sky and flew north. She watched as he flew away, until she could see him no more.

"I would have gladly looked after Tybaris," said General Krylar.

"Thank you, but then I guess you do not fully understand," she said. "There are many who have sought help from Tybaris, but they are never heard. If you are not in the glade, you cannot ask for or give help. Only if the magic that protects her acknowledges you then you are able to help. You may reach the glade, but you would never be permitted in. Unless there is something that I have yet to learn about you."

"I hadn't realised."

"Because of how Tybaris came to be, the magi could not undo what had been cast. The best they could do was give some sort of protection. I chose to stay, but I am not allowed in the glade. Therefore, I have not spoken with Tybaris in a long time."

"But the girl…"

"I know. It is very interesting that she easily walked in there."

"Who is she to be able to do that?"

"I don't know. Maybe it is her gift that allows it. I should go, the others will be waiting." She had now lost sight of the hawk. There was no reason so stay now. Duty called, Miss Quinn would need her in the days to come, that she was certain of.

The others had arrived at the gateway and had to wait for Tyca. Jugra'li explained that once they entered, the gate had to be shut again. It was not safe to keep it open. As always, Quinn needed to know why. The Frenarans lived deep within the depths beneath the mountain and could not pass this point. If they thought the Restar were bad, then they needed to meet the fire wolves that lurked in the shadows. Once they started their journey through the gateway, they could not turn back as they would be closed in. To leave, a bell had to be sounded and that was at least a quarter mile further in the mountain. It had been constructed that way to ensure that there was time to stop the Frenarans if they were following. If they were fortunate enough to have survived first.

Tyca could be seen jogging down the slope towards them. The General had decided to follow and wish them well. He had never been in the tunnels before. It had been too long since they had last been used. Therefore, no reason had existed until now. Now they were assembled, Jugra'li could open the gates. Again, it was obvious why a Frengris was needed, this gate had two handles that had to be pulled inwards to release the latch that locked them. It had been a long time since they had last been touched. They were not moving as he pulled inwards hard. Maybe he had not rested enough before attempting this. He stopped and rested a moment. Quinn walked up to him and looked up at him. Then smiled. He thought that strange.

"Your ancestors would be so proud of you. Especially her," she said.

Jugra'li knew who she referred to. She had been his mate. That was one of the reasons he had left the forest. There was very little that Quinn didn't see when she looked into someone's eyes. Unless you were Marnari. That was a mess that would take time to unravel.

He reached up again and said one word as he pulled the handles inwards. "Fredia."

They heard a snap as the latches clicked in place. The gate was now open. He pushed one side open, just enough to allow them to pass through. Jugra'li looked down at Quinn.

"Thank you," he said.

Quinn gave him one last hug and followed her friends.

Chapter 11

They had been walking for some time. When they had passed through the gateway, they didn't really travel any deeper underground. It was presumed that they were probably deep enough to pass under the mountain. Marnari had concerns though. She had the feeling that they were being watched. Or it might have something to do with being told about the Frenarans. She could just be paranoid right now. Tyca had been watching the shadows, but it was so easy for the mind to play tricks on you in the darkness. Quinn was pleased to be moving forward. She had seen so much and made some new friends. Now she was eager to reach the north and so was leading the party on their way.

"Not too far, Miss Quinn," said Tyca.

"You know you can just call me Quinn, like everyone else. I'm not that important. I have always been on the streets. It was only when Marnari took me as an apprentice that my life started to change," she said, without looking back.

The four were seeming to make good progress. It was hard to tell if the tunnel they walked down was natural or if it had been carved through the mountain.

"I believe the tunnel was partly carved to connect naturally forming areas," said Tyca.

She had been in the dead forest a long time. At times she had been able to converse with those in the gateway city. The recent meeting was not the first time they had seen her or knew of her prowess. Tyca had been the only other person to survive the dead forest and what was more impressive was that she actually lived and survived in the actual forest. It was strange for her to be away from it. The place had been her life for so long. Protecting Tybaris had been her only function. Now she had a new one placed upon her. She glanced forward to look at Quinn.

"She is a curiosity," said Tullan, seeing her stare at Quinn.

"Very much. For her to enter the glade meant that she is more than any mere mortal."

She felt his gaze on her.

"Sorry," she said.

"No. I get it. From what I heard, you have to be a particular type of person to enter."

"Usually, it would only be a magus. She is not. Unless, eventually she will be, perhaps that is why Marnari chose her," said Tyca.

Marnari was trailing behind the others. She was more concerned by the shadows than the conversation. With Tyca there, she knew that she would be looking out for Quinn, which meant that she could concentrate on their safety. She had wanted to use a light spell so that they were able to see better, but had decided to stay with the burning torches they had been provided with. She stopped. Did that rock just more? Or that shadow. No one had really paid attention to the fact that Quinn was a little too far ahead. Then she had to stop though. Something that they had not been told about, the path had been one, now it split to three. She stopped and waited for the others to catch up.

"It would seem we have a problem," said Quinn.

"Wait here," said Tyca.

She moved forward and stepped towards the right path and proceeded along its course. Moments later, she returned.

"That way is impassable. There has been a collapse of the ceiling."

"I have a feeling we are not alone?" said Marnari.

"We aren't," said Tyca.

Before she said more, she glanced towards Quinn, who wasn't there. Looking forwards, she had passed into the dark middle tunnel.

"Quinn," called out Tyca.

"I am alright… Aargh!" came the cry.

Tyca rushed forward as the light from the torch allowed. She stopped, but only just in time. There had been another collapse, but this one led downwards. Tyca paused and looked back.

"I have to follow. You two take the left path and hope we catch up to you later. If not, head out. When I find her, I shall find a way forward."

Marnari knew she would be true to her word and went with Tullan. There was no point all four of them being down the same hole. For a start, it might just be a hole and then they would all be stuck. Tyca dropped down. There was a slight slope and she slid most of the way downwards. It was lighter down here and Quinn was nowhere in sight. The torch made the crystals in the wall surface gleam. It aided her light and she was able to proceed at a quicker pace. Tracks showed that Quinn was moving quickly. Perhaps she hastened to get back to them, which meant that she would not be aware that she had followed. Quinn hadn't needed a torch to see and Tyca was unaware that the walls also had some sort of fluorescent algae on them. This with the crystals gave almost perfect vision in the dimly lit passageway. She had been able to run in the iridescent light and was making good progress and then stopped. The tunnel emerged into a large cavern with stalactite and stalagmites everywhere. She moved through this room slower, taking in all that she saw. There was a pool. She ran her fingers over its surface as she walked through. There was a slope at the other end of the cavern. It led upwards. She started to jog through and up the slope. Tyca still hadn't caught up to her. Those few minutes talking to the others had allowed Quinn to get quite a distance ahead of them.

Now Quinn emerged at the top of the slope into total darkness, but there was a light ahead. At first, she thought it was someone's torch and moved quickly towards it. Quinn soon realised it was not a torch. It was too low and it was more than a single torch flame. The beast walked towards her. He was more than just a simple Frenaran, he was Dirran. Larger and wiser than the others, he had become the alpha of all Frenaran.

"So, we meet," he said.

Quinn stopped; did she know this beast? She tried to look into his eyes, but all she saw was the flames. Dirran turned away.

"That is not allowed, Kokoran."

"What did you call me?"

"Then I guess they have yet to work it out, but I am very old and have lived beyond a century and knew of one before. You will die as she did."

She stepped back from him. He laughed at her.

"Yes, I was the one who took her life. For today you are safe, but if I meet you again, then I will tear out your throat as I did hers."

Now he had met her, he turned to leave.

"Wait, what is a Kokoran?"

"The name that is used for one who can read the soul. Or as some see it, heart-spirit-mind."

"We will meet again. I am sure of it, assuming you reach safety in time. The horde will come now."

Then he was gone. Quinn was still stood there when Tyca found her. "Quinn."

She had not responded to her call and now she was shaking her. Quinn snapped out of it, then looked around.

"Where are the others?"

"They took the other path."

"We have to find them fast; we are all in danger."

The two started to move as quickly as they could and hoped that the tunnel they were in would lead them back to their friends.

Marnari and Tullan had proceeded with caution, based upon what had happened. She was forever watching the shadows and Tullan led them down the tunnel. They had no idea why they had encountered three tunnels. Marnari moved to catch up with Tullan.

"Don't look back, but we have company."

"How many?" he asked.

"One, but I suspect that is a ruse."

The shadow had suddenly started to take form as fire appeared all down its back. Slowly, the beast became engulfed in fire. The Frenarans were fire wolves. Brought up from the depths below and emblazoned with the flames of that, which was beneath. Marnari had been wise not to attack. Most would probably have been scared by a flame beast and lashed out. That would have been a mistake. Eight were lurking in the shadows. As soon as they attacked, they would have been struck down. Now one and many shadows followed. The tunnel was starting to open up, there was a large cavern ahead. Marnari hastened her pace. Tullan caught on quickly, then made the mistake to sneak a glance behind him. The beast saw and as soon as they two's eyes met, the rest started to appear.

"Run!"

Marnari glanced back to see what he meant and now saw nine fire wolves starting to move after them. They would not reach the end of the tunnel before they were on them. There was no choice, but to stop and fight. Tullan drew his sword and Marnari held her hand up and cried, "Vreshna." The wolves fell back, tumbling over each other.

Quinn heard the same word and knew where to go. She turned back and moved to her left. The shadows were hiding the way, but Tyca still had a torch to help her find the path. Quinn held out her hand.

"You will need your bow. Give me the torch."

She knew Quinn was right and did as asked.

"Stay close to me so that I know exactly where you are."

Quinn nodded. Now they moved back towards their friends. The two of them came up behind them. Tullan was not a seasoned veteran or anything like that, but he was just holding his own. Marnari could only keep pushing them back. She couldn't afford to collapse the tunnel otherwise they would have no way back. Then, Tyca started to fire and the Frenarans started to fall one by one. Marnari looked back and saw Quinn was with her.

"Fall back," called Tyca.

They stayed to one side so that Tyca had a clear line of sight. She covered their movements. Slowly, the Frenarans fell, but that was not the end of them. Now they had been dealt with, Tyca could join her friends and move forward, but soon realised why they were still there.

"Like I said, Quinn, we would meet again. Now, come to me so that I can enact your death," said Dirran.

Marnari realised what had happened and saw the symbol of flame in her eyes. Quinn was entranced by the beast's flames. She had stared for too long. Yet, he knew her name. No! They must have met earlier, that is why it had been so easy to control her now.

"Grab her, quickly."

Tullan was the nearest and took hold of Quinn. Marnari looked into her eyes.

"She is lost to you, witch."

All she had was bandages in her bag. She used them to wrap around her head and blind her from the beast's flames.

"Try not to make eye contact with him," she instructed the others.

For Quinn, she was always drawn to the eyes, which is why she was so easily caught. Once Marnari had wrapped and covered Quinn's eyes, she told Tullan to carry her. Tyca was a much better fighter.

"Be ready," warned Marnari.

Tyca understood all too well. She could feel the presence of those in the shadows and was ready, but she wasn't sure when. Marnari stepped forward in front of Tullan and Quinn. Dirran stared into Marnari's eyes. *No. This cannot be.* He was unable to tempt her to the flames. Her eyes were a mess. Marnari saw his hesitation.

"Not so easy looking into my eyes, is it?"

While she had been speaking, she threw her arms out and even though she could not grab them, took control of two large boulders then brought her hands together fast. They slammed, cracked and fell apart, but Dirran had already gone. Now they had another problem. As he disappeared, the shadows became alive. He had no intention of letting them escape. There werc at least twenty. Tyca opened fire immediately. Marnari cried out "Vreshna," to help clear a path for them. She had to get Tullan and Quinn through. Tyca stayed where she was. It was easier to fire from where she was, and as soon as they were on the other side of the Frenarans, she would make her move.

Now she moved. Using her bow as a melee weapon, she started to carve a path through the Frenarans. Dirran had not returned. The witch had stopped and prevented him from dealing with the Kokoran. He would have to find another way. The ends of her bow were scorched. Now that they were through them, Marnari could aid Tyca.

"Don't stop," she told Tullan.

Marnari threw her arms and her whole body into the attack; the beasts were pushed a long way back. If the others had not been around and this hadn't been the gateway, she would have crushed them under tonnes of heavy rock by collapsing the ceiling, but this was such a place that she could not do that. Now they had a few moments to escape. The tunnel was large and wide here, like a tunnel-shaped cavern. They ran.

Chapter 12

Once the Frenarans had recovered, they gave chase. Tyca could have stopped and held them back whilst the others escaped, but it was unclear how many more lurked in the shadows and had not yet revealed themselves. Until they allowed the fire to consume and cover their bodies, you were unaware of them. She feared that there could be hundreds there. It was more sensible to stay close to the others. At least then, if they were attacked, they could work together. Tullan was still carrying Quinn. In those few brief moments, the alpha must have found her and started to sow the seed so that he would have control over her. She was not infallible. The girl needed to find a way to be able to protect herself against such things, but was that even possible? When you looked into someone's eyes with the gift that she had, how would you even know what you might uncover? If she ever met a magus who wanted to take control or advantage of her, the fate could be just as bad.

"Will she recover?" asked Tullan.

"I have no idea. This is all new to me," said Marnari.

There efforts should be more focused on escaping, not talking.

Ahead, something was shimmering on the floor. The walls were widening. They were now approaching what looked like a large underground lake.

"We have to get to the lake," called Marnari. "Even if they can swim, they will not be able to sustain their fire."

They hastened the pace. The beasts knew what was ahead. Now, the walls came alive. Marnari could not believe how many had been hiding in the shadows; it was like the whole of the wall had literally been lit with fire.

"Faster," called Tyca.

Her bow would be no good if they attacked, so she slung it over her torso and drew a long dagger from her back. It was different to the ones at her waist.

"Is that?" Marnari started to say.

"Yes. It is the Vishra."

The Vishra was a dagger that had been created during the great war. The Krykarins had used dark magic, one that had been difficult to combat. The order of magi had no choice but to consult ancient scriptures and so many things had been created or born from the old magic. Very few knew how to use it correctly or even wisely. Tybaris had been created using the same ancient magic, but in the hands of an apprentice who sealed the fate of Tybaris to the forest for eternity. The Vishra had also been created, but in the hands of Kalakar, a wiser, more noble magus. The weapon was only to be used in extreme circumstances and never on a mortal man or beast. It was said to hold a strong magic and would combat the same. Now, Tyca held it in her hand. The blade would destroy the beasts with a mere prick of its tip, but in her hand, she could probably kill them all if necessary.

"You know what will happen if you use it?" said Marnari.

"Yes."

The blade, as strong as it was, came with a price. Not one to the user, but for the length and time of its use. If she used it, then they would certainly all die, but then the blade, once its power vanished, would need one year to regain its power. The blade did not become stronger the less you used it or the longer it was sheathed. It didn't work that way, but Tyca had sworn to protect Quinn. She would, if necessary, give her life for her, just as she would have for Tybaris. They continued to run. A Frenaran jumped towards them, knowing the importance of such a dagger, Marnari pushed the beast away. It would be such a waste for one. As soon as she used that blade, it's power would start to ebb, which meant to take full advantage of its power Tyca would have to engage them all.

"We are nearly at the lake, what do I do with Quinn?" asked Tullan.

He was concerned that she might drown or be hurt if they dived in. A decision had been made for Tyca; she sheathed the Vishra and took Quinn from Tullan.

"Keep up," she said, as her pace quickened.

The lake looked still and tranquil ahead of them. They had no idea what it really was. The beasts were off the walls and running alongside them. Tullan swiped at them as best as he could with his sword as they ran. Marnari could only push one or two back, they were almost sprinting. How could Tyca run as quick as she did with Quinn in her arms too? Marnari had heard many tales of the huntress, but didn't really know who she was or where she came from. There was even a pack on her back too, although it didn't look heavy, unless she was that strong. The lake was only about fifty feet away from them, but they were tiring and slowing down. The Frenarans didn't seem to tire. If these had been on the surface chasing Tybaris, then it would have been really interesting.

The surface of the lake was starting to move. Until now not even a ripple had stirred. Now, it was like a stone had been thrown into the centre of the lake as ripples were moving outwards from the centre. They were getting larger as the centre of the lake started to rise upwards. What was this? Was this also part of the Frenarans' plans to force them to the lake's edge for one last trap? The group stopped. They feared that they were now trapped and there was no escape. The surface of the water stopped and a creature appeared as the water slipped back to the lake's surface. The creature was a making of the water itself.

"A sprite," called Tyca.

She was old, considering she had been around since the great war and knew many things. The sprite was only as large as Quinn and moved across the water's surface. It was able to move and do anything whilst on or in the water, but if it stepped onto the land, its time was short before it needed to return and its abilities would be greatly hindered.

Lyrinia was the sprite of the brine lake. A lake that had been formed as the land had cracked and the tunnel that formed the gateway between two continents became damaged and vulnerable from the beasts in the depths below. The Krykarins had hoped that by releasing the beasts, they would have an advantage to be able to move easily north and south. The facture brought more than they bargained for and the lake had been formed. The pinnacle that the range of mountains sat on, extended out from the mainland and curved to the left as it ran from the land. It had been hard to navigate and sail around and only the foolhardy attempted such a task, as the storms had been known to throw the ships on the rocky base of the mountain's pinnacle. Such a formation was fragile, which is why the Krykarins had intended to use the tunnel. It was easy for them to cause damage to the tunnels beneath, but this had allowed the ocean waters to enter too and the lake was formed.

They were in danger and it looked like they feared her too, but then she hadn't had visitors in so very long. Right now, though, there was no time for pleasantries. The Frenarans would be on them in moments. She had no choice. Lyrinia stepped out of the lake. Tyca watched in awe as she raised her arms high above her head. That wasn't what had caught her eyes. The movement of her arms brought forth a huge wave behind her. It was so tall that it was almost like a wall. You could not even see across the lake to the other side. Lyrinia recognised the huntress.

"Huntress," she said, bowing her head. "Do you still have the blade?"

She knew of its existence too. Marnari was confused. What was happening? How did they know each other? There was so much that she still didn't know. With the order gone, she was alone. She had learned a lot from her mentor, but it would seem that much of the land and the past had been kept from her.

"I do."

"Take hold of it by the sheath and plunge the hilt into the ground and then remove the sheath. Hurry, I cannot sustain this for much longer. If I falter, they will end us all."

Tyca ripped the bindings on her back as she pulled it forward and did as she asked. She was unsure about what was going to happen. This was even new to her. As soon as Lyrinia saw the blade, she moved her arms over her head and forward. The tidal wave from the lake came racing forward. It passed over them all yet they weren't even wet. The blade had protected them from the strong brine water. The Frenarans were too close and had not expected this. They started to scatter, but some were too close. The brine negated the effects of the flames, but to the Frenarans, it was almost like pouring a strong acid over the skin. It stripped away the fire in mere seconds and then attacked the beast. She had only enough time to scatter and stop them. Lyrinia would now have to retreat. Tyca reclaimed the blade from the ground and picked up Quinn. She was still out from the effects of Dirran. They started to wade into the lake. Yet as they walked, it didn't seem very deep. Marnari suspected there was magic at work. The brine waters came from the ocean. It couldn't just be a shallow pool. Lyrinia had retreated to the depths she needed to replenish herself. It was hard to do what she had. Before parting, she had told them she would return and not to leave. They would be safe on the other side of the lake. The Frenarans could not swim in the brine. It would kill them.

She vanished as they reached the other side. Her presence was needed to allow them to walk across. If she had not been there then they would have had to swim, but as the girl was not able to swim then she had to lend them her aid one more time, before she slept. Now they could catch their breaths and rest. All were concerned about Quinn and didn't really know what affect Dirran had been able to do to her. She still slept. The others decided to do the same, but Marnari had so many questions that she would very much like answers to. Things that had been quiet and dormant for a very long time had woken and were coming together once again. Tybaris and the huntress, with her shadow hawk. The Vilhar still lived in the city. Not all had succumbed to the forest. Then the return of the Frengris, the last finally having the courage to return home, and now they had met Frenarans and the water sprite. The keeper and protector of the brine lake. Marnari looked down at Quinn. She realised one very important fact. That none of what she had witnessed in the last few weeks would have been possible or seen, or even come to be if it had not been for this one girl. When she had first encountered her in the capital, she sat there as if she owned that plinth, shouting out to those around her and realising that there was something intriguing and interesting about her. But what she didn't realise was how far her gift would take her and reveal all those that she encountered to be so much more. Even though Marnari was unable to read her, because of what she had seen and learned in life that had scrambled her soul so much, Marnari realised that she only knew a fraction. Whereas Quinn could see and know everything. Especially, if she looked into the souls of all those that existed and there was an eternal amount that could exist. Quinn was far more precious and important than she had first realised, but the alpha Frenaran knew immediately who she was; the Kokoran as he called her. She had almost been lost to them all. He had faced her twice, the first to entice, the second to entrap. If he had succeeded, what would have been achieved? It had been important enough to have so many come after them. Only one had existed before and he had killed them too. She could easily see how they had succumbed. Many times, she had stared into the flames of a fire. Their almost hypnotic dance. Lulling you to a place of peace and calm. Teasing your eyelids to close and sleep. Yet that was only one side of the flame. The other was its destructive and damaging nature, how it could suddenly dance, quickly and harshly. Leaving the safety of the fire and leap out at anything around it and then grab hold of whatever it touched and destroy in a matter of moments. Or at least damaging and charring the surface of what it touched. Leaving behind a scar to remember.

Quinn had been lucky that they had all been there. Part of her was afraid to remove the bandage from Quinn's eyes. More because lying on the far shore was a solitary large Frenaran. It just lay there in the darkness, hidden away. She had seen it appear as the waters had become tranquil again. It was as black as a moonless night on the other side, but she knew he was still there. Watching and waiting.

Chapter 13

Lyrinia returned the next day and stood on the northern side of the shore. All were up and active, except Quinn.

"I came to ensure you were all safe and unharmed. That is why I asked you to wait and it was wise you rested before continuing your journey. What is wrong with the girl?" asked Lyrinia.

"She has looked into the eyes of the alpha," said Marnari.

"I see, how many times?"

"Twice."

"Then she will not wake as he now owns her. That is why he lurks on the other side of the lake. All he needs is to look in her eyes again and you will not be able to stop her crossing this lake and going to her death."

"Three time's the charm," mumbled Tullan.

"Precisely, but not in a good way. The charming manner of the flame spells her doom."

She turned around and faced the southern shore. It was pitch black. "You cannot have her Dirran, she is mine now."

The others could not see if she was actually talking to anyone or whether it was just a dark empty space. Lyrinia sensed he had not moved. Now she reached down with her hand and scooped up a ball of water. Similar to the ones that

Quinn had created to play with the dolphin. Then she threw it south. A flame briefly emerged as Dirran scarpered from where she had thrown. Then, he was lost in the darkness again.

Lyrinia ignored Marnari. She didn't know her, but she did know Tyca. "Huntress, would you permit me to take the girl?"

"Why?" asked Marnari.

Lyrinia turned her gaze to her. She was surprised that she had spoken. "And you are?"

"Marnari Rashna, last magus of the order of magi."

"I see. I am unfamiliar with you. I had believed that all of them had either perished or ran."

"Ran?"

"Yes. You just said you were the last. If they are not dead, then they still live, but elsewhere."

"So, why do they not return to help?"

"Are you able to tell them what has transpired?"

"No."

"Then they may not know."

She turned her attention away from Marnari and looked at Tyca. Then extended her arms.

"You cannot aid her," said Lyrinia.

Tyca lifted her from the ground. Lyrinia had not left the lake this time. She needed to conserve her energy for what was about to happen. She had Quinn in her arms and had moved back to the centre of the lake.

"Dragon of the sea, come forth and aid me."

She repeated this twice more before the water started to bubble and froth. Then a snake-like beast of water emerged from the deep depths. Its watery face resembled a close likeness to the fabled dragons that had never been seen or considered existed, except in travellers' tales. It saw Quinn in her arms and leaped from the lake and then dived back down, passing over Quinn, who was consumed as his mouth engulfed her and the two of them were gone.

"I need to leave you now. She will be safe. Farewell."

Then Lyrinia dived down and under the surface of the lake.

"What about Quinn?" said Marnari, staring at the tranquil surface of the lake.

She was gone and so was Quinn. Marnari had no idea what was expected of them now. Tyca could see the concern on her face.

"She is safe. Lyrinia will not harm her. She will do everything she can to heal her eyes. If she can't, then Quinn is in danger."

"How do you know this? What else is there about you that we don't know?" said Marnari.

She was on the attack. Angry with everything that had happened and Tyca had just become her target to release it all. Tyca stood unwavering in front of her and when Marnari was close enough, she placed a hand on her shoulder.

"She will be fine and as to who I am, you already know I am the huntress. My task is to protect and Tybaris knew that, which is why she chose me as Quinn's protector. It was my first time facing the Frenarans, but I have met Lyrinia before. The tunnel was damaged during the great war."

She related the details of how it had happened and then how she had come to meet Lyrinia.

"I had one last time to enter the tunnels. By then the lake had appeared. I elected myself to survey and check the tunnel one last time before it was sealed again. I sat for a while on the edge of its shore. Lyrinia appeared. Even though I had never met such a creature, I was not afraid. It was strange, but I guess with everything that happened during the great war, nothing really surprises me anymore. I guess with the order disbanding, you had not learned of what happened then."

"I was an apprentice then, but you seldom got to know important things. I was still learning and I guess I still am."

Lyrinia was following her dragon. She called it a dragon as she had once sat on the dock shores and listened to the tales told and liked the sound of what she heard. All sprites had such a water beast; it was how they were able to travel long distances. The sprite form she used was as close as she could get to being mortal. In that form, she could be hurt or worse, removed from existence. Right now, she didn't have far to go. There was a sanctuary under the pinnacle. It was her home when she wasn't guarding the gateway tunnel. She had chosen it as her task. Lyrinia had always been curious about the other races that lived on the surface. The tales had tempted her many times. Alas, she did not realise that the tunnels were to be sealed. Tyca had been the last surfacer that she had spoken to. The ocean king wouldn't let her change assignment. It had to fall to someone and as she had almost begged for it at the time, was now tasked to be there forever.

She didn't need to merge with the dragon as it was only a short distance to her home. They reached the cave beneath and went in through the watery tunnel and emerged in a brine pool. Lyrinia stepped onto the surface and took Quinn from him. "You can rest now, thank you for coming."

When he was not at her side, he resided here. He rolled over as if lying down on the surface of the pool. Lyrinia carried Quinn up a few steps to the inner sanctum of her home.

It was simple, mostly water covered walls and some weed or bright colour coral. She was a creature of the ocean and so had a simple meagre life. In the centre of the sanctum was another pool, this one was different. For a start, it was smaller, almost like a bathing pool, and it had freshwater infused with minerals from the ocean depths that naturally formed here below the surface.

Now, she carefully removed Quinn's bandages from her eyes.

"I am sorry for what I am about to do, but it is necessary if you are to recover."

Quinn was still not conscious. Lyrinia just presumed she could still hear.

"I am afraid that I have to drown you. The water needs to completely fill you to ensure that all trace of Dirran is expelled from your system. I know that you will wake instantly and your first reaction will be to fight to survive. I will have no choice, but to hold you under. You will understand once you have drowned."

Lyrinia entered the pool too. The brine that had been within her form disappeared and she became one with the pool. With one quick dive she plunged beneath the surface with Quinn still in her arms. As she had said, Quinn awoke. Her hands were flying around in the water. She was wanting to reach the surface. Quinn had never learned to swim before and this was like a nightmare. The water was rushing into the mouth, she wanted it out. "Oh, please." Her mind screamed. Then, after several minutes of thrashing around she became still. Quinn had drowned.

Lyrinia released her and spoke.

"You can open your eyes now."

Quinn did as the words said. The fire had gone from her eyes and she was again Quinn, but she felt very strange.

"How is this possible?" she asked.

She tried to look into Lyrinia's eyes, but there was nothing to see. Not that she didn't exist, but she didn't exist like mortals. She was made of water and so Quinn was unable to read anything from her eyes. That was a first.

"This pool is very special. If I had done this in any other type of water, then you would have drowned. This pool simulates the effect. Your body needed to be filled with the water to cleanse itself of the effects that Dirran had over you. I know you have a gift, but never look into the eyes of a demon."

"Demon?" she asked.

"I guess it's the only word that really fits. We are from the depths of the ocean called sprites. The Frenarans are from the depths of the land and are therefore know as demons by mortals. The Krykarins worship such creatures and had hoped to harness their power in the great war, but that kind of thing comes at a very heavy price. The Krykarin shaman that summons the quake to disrupt the fabric of the mountain thought he could control the beasts, but he couldn't and so paid the ultimate price."

"Why are you telling me all of this?"

"Because you need to learn if you are to survive. You are Kokoran, reader of mortal souls. It is a very rare gift and you need to embrace it as you face the challenges of each day. You are on a journey to find an heir. I listened to your friends last night; I was only under the surface resting and recharging, but the sound of their voices created vibrations across the surface, which allow me to eavesdrop on their conversation. I learned a lot."

"Are they safe?" she asked, suddenly realising she had left them behind.

"Yes. I ensured they were before I brought you here."

"How long do I have to stay submerged in this pool?" asked Quinn.

"Until we finish talking."

Lyrinia hadn't spoken to anyone in a long time. She intended to make the most of her time with Quinn. It made a nice change for her. She knew her friends would not leave without her and Quinn was perfectly safe now she had deliberately drowned her. She told her one or two things about the great war, but only from what little she had encountered and heard about whilst residing in the lake. Even then, that knowledge was limiting as she had only been in the lake a short while and the war was slowly coming to an end. Quinn tried to ask her if she knew anything about her. There was so much she didn't know. Having lost a mother and then the old lady abandoning her. She had been alone most of her life. Even though there had been others in the city, they were mostly passers-by and were not real friends. Over time, she had learned names of those she saw regularly, it sometimes made it seem more friendly if she called someone by a name, but they were still not her friend. Now she had Marnari, Tullan, Jugra'li, Tybaris, Tyca and now Lyrinia. She didn't mind staying. It was nice to have the conversation with her too.

They started to emerge from the pool.

"Now, as you exit, the air will want to take control of your lungs. As you rise, breathe out."

"But I have no breath."

"I know, but try, you will be expelling the water from your body. You need to force as much out as you can. Then it will be easier to spit out the last of the water and take in air."

Quinn tried as instructed and swam up. Lyrinia also had to give her instructions on how to swim. The two rose to the surface. It was not easy to swim and expel the water. They stopped just below the surface. Lyrinia gave her a hug to help force more out and then when she felt Quinn was ready, helped to pull her up and into the air. Her body wanted to convulse. Quinn's body felt like it was still drowning as she still had water in her body.

"Spit it out," called Lyrinia.

Quinn was trying so hard. Then there was enough room for some air to enter and the balance of the water was ejected. She lay on the surface of the sanctum floor, breathing hard. It felt so good.

"I will need to take you back to your friends so that you can resume your journey."

"Am I safe from Dirran?"

"I don't know. The last Kokoran died. The only advice I can give you is this. Are you able to recall the souls you have seen really fast? If you can, then it will be like looking into the eyes of many all at once. When you read a soul, you use your eyes and it is your soul that connects you to them, as it did with Dirran. If you can rotate many souls through your mind at once. Then your eyes will reflect that. He will not be able to read your soul. At least, that is my theory, because he can only kill you if he has control of your soul."

"I think I understand. I will have to practice. Thank you, Lyrinia. You're a good friend."

Lyrinia had never been called friend before. No such word existed for a sprite, but she had heard the word on the surface and understood its meaning. For Quinn to call her friend meant a lot.

"One last thing before I take you back."

She went and opened a small clam shell and took out a pearl and handed it to Quinn. The pearl was strange; it wasn't black or white. It was red.

"Why is it red?"

"When the Frenarans tore the shaman apart that had released them from the depths, I was later able to collect a single drop of his blood and trap it in a pearl. I didn't know if it would ever be useful. Krykarin shamans are very powerful. You may find a use for it one day. If not, then it will be a reminder of our time together."

Quinn placed the pearl in her tunic pocket and closed it shut. It would be safe there.

"Now I want you to meet my dragon," said Lyrinia.

She clapped her hands several times to wake him up. Quinn had been out on the trip down. The water dragon rolled over and stared at them both.

"You need to take Quinn back," she said. "Don't give me that look. You mostly sleep each day. It isn't like I ask a lot of you these days."

Quinn was unable to see any change in the dragon's face, while she spoke. "You will need to jump in and let him swallow you."

Her eyes went wide at the thought of being swallowed by a dragon. "How do you think you got here?"

Quinn climbed into the ocean waters.

"Hold your breath before you go under, this isn't the pool. Once he has swallowed, you will be fine and safe."

The dragon made a noise within the water.

"No, you will take her back alone, I am tired and need to rest. When you get to the surface, just spit her out."

The surface of the water made more noise.

"The two of you will be fine. Now off with you, I will see you when you return."

Quinn dived down and the dragon leapt out of the water and re-emerged over the top of her, engulfing her in one swallow. He then raced back to the surface, showing off on his way by twisting and turned as he went. Quinn had no idea how she was not drowning. The dragon was made entirely of sea water. Yet had shape and form. They eventually arrived at the brine lake and as soon as his mouth hit the surface, he spat her out. She skimmed across the surface for a brief second and then gathered herself together and swam to the shore. The dragon had already gone. Her friends stood watching the sudden entrance.

"Hello," she said. "Sorry I have been gone so long."

Tyca reached out and hugged her. Then Marnari and even Tullan. They prepared her some food from what little they had and then set off north. From here, it was a very long walk.

Chapter 14

It was a couple of weeks later, the journey under the ocean was a long trek. They could easily have used their mounts here, that would have shortened the journey considerably. The gateway city didn't have mounts. With the problems of the Restar and how overgrown the dead forest was, it would have been cruel to have kept such a beast there, as it would never be used or allowed to roam. Quinn missed not having Clara with her. She was a very well-tempered horse and after Quinn had spoken with her, had been very kind as it was her first time on a horse. She hoped that Clara had been sensible enough to follow Marnari's horse. It occurred to Quinn that she had no idea where Marnari actually lived and what her new home would be, once they had actually found the heir to the throne. Yet, it was still unclear, until they found Crellis, if he existed. If he did, where was he, that would be a trek too. The more she thought about it the more she wondered if she would ever see Clara again.

The gate at the other end didn't require a Frengris, it was opened with lower levers. When they had eventually decided to gate this end, a Frengris had been taken from the equation. Tyca was familiar with the mechanism and easily opened the gate. They had been underground for so long that the light literally blinded them; they were seeing objects before their eyes for a while until their sight re-accustomed. Tyca had rang the bell, which was the tradition for the traveller using the tunnels. It notified those on the surface to open the gate. She had been surprised to open the gate herself.

Now that her eyes had cleared, it became clear why no one had opened the gate. The city at this end was deserted.

"I would like to welcome you to land of the Hytertans, but it would seem that there is no welcome. Much has changed since the last time I was here."

"When was the last time you were here?" asked Marnari.

"Not since I took an oath to protect Tybaris. So, many years," she replied.

"A lot can definitely happen in that time. The gateway has not been used for so long that they probably left thinking that it was no longer of use. Especially if they had learned the tales of the Frenarans and loss of Frengris. They would have been able to enter and not exit. It would have been a wasted journey," concluded Marnari.

"True."

They started to walk around the old deserted city. Doors were flapping and banging every now and then as the passing breeze caught hold of them. It was cold here. The land of the Hytertans was mostly snow and ice. The southern region of the land was still a mix of life and growth mixed with more seasonal cold weather, but where they needed to go was permanent snow and ice. The change in temperature was already affecting Quinn. Tyca noticed her with arms around her chest, trying to keep warm. Marnari had not thought about the journey ahead and didn't think about needing something warmer. It was just presumed that Crellis was at the capital as he was a former General. She took her pack from her back, set it down and opened to find an item inside. The pack wasn't really heavy. At the bottom was the item she needed.

"Put this on, it will help."

"Thank you," said Quinn.

She handed her a black cloak. As soon as she took it, she could feel how very soft it was. It was unlike the simple traveller cloaks that were coarse and sometimes irritable. This reminded her of those worn by the Lords and Ladies in the king's court at the capital of Rhutra. Quinn glanced up at Tyca once she had wrapped it around her. She could immediately tell the difference and was warmer already.

"It trails on the ground," she said.

Tyca smiled. Quinn had never seen her smile before. She moved forward and took hold of some drawstrings at the top, on the back of the cloak, and carefully pulled them and then tied them in a bow. The drawstrings were red. Odd for a black cloak. "That's interesting," said Quinn.

Seeing the cloak shrink.

"It was made for me by my sister. I wasn't aware of this until she started to borrow it. The red was meant to resemble her and the black for me. She would always call me her shadow protector and she was the scarlet princess. It's how I became to be named the shadow huntress."

"I'm sorry about what happened to your sister."

Tyca forgot that Quinn was aware of what happened, but that was between them. "You may borrow it, like she did. When we find a town or village, we will need to gather more so we can travel north."

Quinn had been following her to the city wall and they were both now stood on the ramparts looking out.

"No," said Tyca.

"What?" said Quinn.

It was not clear to her what had happened. All she could see was a herd of sleeping beasts scattered across the ground about fifty metres from the wall, but circling all the way around.

"Shinra, they are predatory savage beasts. This changes things. Either they forced the residents out or have moved here as it is abandoned. We need to find the others." Quinn was still unsure why this would be a problem. Marnari was just walking around. She too had been concerned about Quinn and the cold, but had been unable to find anything that would help. The place had been completely cleaned out. It was obvious that no one would be coming back.

Tullan was tired from the long walking. He so wished he owned a horse. It would have saved him having to walk everywhere, but he had not been fortunate enough to own one. Now he was sat, resting his tired aching body. In the time they had been in the tunnel, it had been nothing but walking. It was nice to be out in the light again. The tunnel, if it was to be used on a regular basis, could really do with extra lighting.

"Where is Marnari?" said Tyca, appearing.

A short, hooded figure followed close behind her. She was rather snug and cosy wrapped in the cloak.

"Where did you get that?" he asked Quinn, whilst pointing a direction for Tyca. "It's Tyca's. Her sister made it for her a long time ago. She let me borrow it." Quinn carried on. Tullan pulled his boots back on, it had been good to air his feet. The well had dried up, otherwise he would have washed them too, they certainly needed it.

Tyca eventually found her rummaging through junk and dusty muck. "Marnari, I require your presence," she said.

She could tell from her voice that it was a matter of urgency. Tyca didn't even wait for a response and turned around and started to mount the city wall at the nearest point. Marnari followed. She had no idea what had got Tyca all riled up. When she caught up to her, she was gazing north over the ramparts. More than a hundred Shinra lay sleeping. They were large four-legged, furred beasts that usually preferred the cold and harshness of the land further north. They had sharp claws and teeth to match. Shinra were savage hunting beasts. Their size did make them slow, and they usually hunted in small groups, but were not a pack creature. Yet so many made her think differently. Something must have changed for them to be so far south.

Marnari stood next to her. She knew very little of the beast and didn't even know what one looked like, so was unaware of what she was looking at.

"What was so urgent?" she asked.

"I guess you don't know, these are Shinra."

She then explained about the savageness of the beast and how they normally hunted and their territorial behaviour. Marnari was starting to understand her concern.

"The beasts will wake during the night. It is late, therefore, we are here for the night."

"But we are in the city. Why the concern?"

"They eat flesh and don't usually care about the source. When they wake, their first instinct will be to hunt for food."

Again, Marnari could not understand the concern. As they were talking, the sun was declining in the west and it would soon be time for the Shinra to wake. Marnari's face looked vague as she looked at Tyca.

"For a magus, you know very little."

"I have mostly kept to Rhutra."

"We are a viable food source. The Shinra will be able to smell us even in the city. I checked the gates. They will not hold such a number."

Now she realised what the problem was. They were trapped inside the city and could potentially be the Shinra's next meal.

"What do you propose?"

"We need to return beyond the gateway. Hopefully, they will not detect us there."

Now the sun had dipped out of sight. The beasts were stirring as the cold night air rippled across the fur on their backs. One was suddenly heard roaring in the centre of the herd. A second growled at it and was immediately slapped to the ground. The two then engaged in a vicious fight.

"It would seem the don't much care for each other," said Marnari, observing the fight.

"We need to move," said Tyca.

Quinn and Tullan had waited on the ground. She had not wanted to climb the dirty, dusty ladder while wearing cloak and Tullan just didn't see the point. The two dropped down and Tyca headed back towards the gateway. Marnari turned to see Quinn dressed and wrapped in the cloak. She placed a hand on her head and felt the softness of the cloak.

"Where did you get that?" she asked.

"It is Tyca's, she lent it to me."

She ran her hand over the fabric again. Something of this quality was only usually used by someone who was highborn.

Her eyes looked towards Tyca. She knew her as the shadow huntress, but had only recognised her as such when she saw the black hawk. Who was she really? Or before being the huntress? There was no time to dwell right now. More beasts could be heard waking. They picked up the pace.

Tyca was almost back at the gateway.

Then Tyca waited for them to catch up and then opened the gate. They all entered. She had grabbed pieces of broken furniture. Sufficient to have a fire burning all night. Once they were all back inside, she closed the gate, but didn't lock it. The first thing she did was build a large fire with the pieces she had dragged in. Each of them, seeing what she was doing, grabbed more. Between them they should have sufficient to last the night. Then she went further into the tunnel alone.

"I will be back shortly."

Then left. No one had a chance to comment. She was familiar with this region. The way she spoke, addressed and seemed to know the land, had suggested to Marnari that she had definitely been here before. Maybe even lived here for a while.

It was several minutes later before Tyca returned. They could smell her before they saw her. She had been digging in the ground, the air was not just stale because no fresh air came into the tunnel. it was from the ground. This was why she had gone further into the tunnel. She had dug down to find the rotting smell that was in the ground and had rubbed it across the outside of her garments.

"Oh, that is foul," said Tullan. "Why did you do that?"

"For protection. It was the only thing I could think of," replied Tyca.

“Why do you need protection, are you expecting them to get in?” asked Quinn, a little concerned.

Her hands had not been covered. She wanted to be able to hold her weapons without the stuff on her hands. Tyca placed a hand on the top of Quinn’s head. She looked up.

“They will never get in,” she said, reassuringly.

Removing her hand, she walked to the gate and opened it slightly and exited. Before anyone could say anything, she had gone and then they heard the click of the mechanism as she locked them in.

“NO!” exclaimed Quinn.

Chapter 15

The night had been uneventful, but Tyca took her responsibilities seriously. To protect one meant that she needed to protect all. The sun was rising, its warmth touched her face and woke her. Tyca had been sat in front of the gate all night. She knew that they would not be able to get in, that wasn't why she had done it. If they had caught their scent and broken the gates, then they could easily have been sleeping on the streets when they came out today. Plus, she also wanted to be able to see the sun come up. They would need time to leave the city and make their exit from here. Tyca stood and stretched. It had not been comfortable sleeping in a seated position on the outside of the gate. She unlocked the gate and opened it to enter again. Now she woke the others and asked them to keep their voices low and quiet. It was time and the Shinra had only just settled down for their sleep.

Tyca hastened to the front gate and unbarred it. She had no idea how it had been barred from the inside. Unless they had climbed down over the wall. That wasn't actually a bad idea. Tyca chose not to open the gate and enact the new idea that had just come to her. She had seen plenty of rope. The others were told to follow the city wall to the east end and she would meet them there. Seeing the Shinra and knowing what they were capable of didn't make it any better for them even though they were asleep. They all moved cautiously and slowly. None of them wanting to make a sound so they did as instructed. Tyca had already dropped over the wall. She left the rope in place. It was unclear as to what route they would need to return.

Now she led the way. East was the only option at his point. To go in any other direction meant creeping through the herd of Shinra. That was not a viable option considering the group she was with. If she had been on her own, then she would have taken her chances and passed through them going north. If her memory served her correctly, there used to be a fishing village on the eastern coast. The point where the gate was meant that it was about a day away. They had been walking for weeks now. Much more was necessary if they were to get to the capital in the north of Hyterta. No one spoke for a long time. They hadn't dared whilst in range of the Shinra. Tyca hadn't washed. She had hoped the smell would be strong enough to mask them all.

"Where are we going?" asked Marnari, moving to be alongside Tyca.

Quinn was in the middle as normal, still wrapped in a nice warm cloak. She was the only one. The others kept moving. It was another reason for being up early. At least with the sun out, the air was less cold. They needed to be at the village before nightfall. It was a trek. The land was mostly rock and dry earthen areas. Breezes blowing down from the north usually dried up any moisture in the surface of the ground. Some things seemed to grow there, but not a vast number of crops. They mostly hunted for food and furs. They then traded with the markets in Uboria. There were several ports that welcomed the trade from Hyterta. A lot of what they grew were root-based and were hardy in the cold conditions. There were a lot of hills.

What little grass the land had was short. It didn't seem to grow tall. There were many trees, which was good for the Hytertans as it meant they would always be warm at night. Now the group had moved slightly north to cut across the south-eastern corner of the land.

"There should be a small fishing village in the eastern coast," she replied.

"You have been to Hyterta before I take it, as you seem to know so much," enquired Marnari.

Tyca had not really spoken about herself. It seemed one had to draw answers out of her as she forwarded very little.

"I have spent time here."

It was all she said. That didn't give Marnari a lot to work with. Either Tyca didn't like to talk and so was vague with answers or she didn't want others to know about her.

"Have you been to this village before?" she continued.

"No."

That question didn't help. Tyca was hard work, although Quinn liked her, but then Quinn seemed to like everyone. The group had no choice, but to follow Tyca. She had a quick pace, not fast, but you tired after a time. Tyca knew the importance of getting to the village sooner than later. She was used to the weather and terrain, they were not. Quinn would be fine in her cloak. She reached the top of a small slope and looked to the north-east.

"There," she called.

Out on the horizon you could just make out the peaks of wooden-structured roof tops.

"How long?" asked Tullan.

They hadn't walked this fast in the tunnels. Tyca lifted her head, the breeze caught her fast.

"It is earlier than I expected," she said.

"What is?" asked Marnari.

"The north wind. I had not expected it to arrive until nearly dusk. This will not be good for you two. Either we find shelter to protect you from its chill or we press on, but we won't have the warmth of a fire."

"Press on," said Marnari. "Our movements should keep us warm."

"I am sure my feet will give out before then," said Tullan.

"Too bad," said Tyca, "because then you would be left behind. If the chill gets too much then we will all die if we try to carry you."

Tullan did not like that idea and Tyca seemed a little harsh with her words. Marnari saw it for concern, where Tullan was unsure. He was cold and tired. This was about his limit. He had not realised that this adventure would be so hard and taxing. Right now, he longed for a hot bath in Uboria.

They pressed on, the wind was strong, but held back allowing them to move forward. It was still bad enough; the wind was icy and they were so ill-equipped. The light was starting to fade; they would not make it. Even though she could see the buildings more clearly in the village ahead, it was clear that the rest could not maintain the pace. There was a gulley nearby. A quick examination showed that it went to a dead end.

"I am sorry, but you are too slow; you will need to take shelter and huddle together. Quinn, the cloak please."

They settled down and she laid the cloak over them all like a blanket, with Quinn in the middle.

"I shall try to be as quick as I can."

With that, she was gone. She just had to hope she could find them again. Tyca started to snap branches as she passed them, it was the only way that she could mark her path back to them. The light was dim, all she had to mark her way was the lights of the village ahead. She moved as quickly as she could. The light was fading faster and then it was gone.

Tyca eventually arrived at the village. The door burst open as she entered the tavern. The wind howling behind them.

"Inn keeper," she called.

There was too much noise from the volume in the tavern, they were all there to warm themselves by the tavern's large fire. She pushed her way through the crowd. The longer she waited, the worse her friends would be. Picking up an empty tankard at the bar counter, she rapped it hard on the surface. The inn started to quieten.

"I need help and assistance," she called. "I have three that I travel with that are huddled in the winds a few miles out. They are too tired to get here without assistance. I need cloaks and a means to help them back. Who will assist?"

"They are probably already dead," came a cry from the back.

"What happened to the northern hospitality? Did the north wind come down and steal from you while you slept?"

One stepped forward.

"I guess you're not from these parts. Things have changed a lot."

She glanced over and looked at him.

"I used to be from here and there was a time that the people would rally together and help one another. What changed?"

"Frekrikans."

She stopped in her tracks. Tyca knew them only too well. Was this why Crellis had come north to lend a hand with his years of knowledge and experience? The Frekrikans were a rival, cold race, that lived north and east of the Hyterta lands. She had no idea what had brought them to these shores, but she would aim to find out whilst she was here.

"It would seem I have been away too long," she said, her face looked sad. There was only one other way she may get help, under the circumstances. She reached into her pack and pulled out a coin purse.

"I take it, even with all the changes, that sovereigns are still used as a currency in these parts," she called.

Tyca was in desperate need of help. The sovereign was a rare currency and only came from one place. Heads turned in her direction.

"It is still a currency accepted by the people here, but they are rarely seen," came a voice.

She produced a silver sovereign and held it up.

"I will give this to the one who will aid me and provide me what I need to aid my friends."

"The only way you could have got that was to steal it. They are never given to the public these days."

It would seem much had changed.

"Get the thief."

A tall, thick-set, dark-skinned man stood up from behind her and stepped to her side.

"You all know me, I am Ufanari. Anyone so much as step forward, I will knock them into next week."

The room went quiet.

"I will help," he said. "But not for the coin."

"Can you get the items I need?"

He nodded and beckoned for her to follow him. Then he went to a warehouse and entered. Ufanari was a trader and had all she needed. Regardless of his need, she left the sovereign on the counter. He would find it when it was light. She took nothing for free. The two set off; he had hand torches lit and the cloaks to help her friends.

They eventually found the trail she marked.

"It would seem you are well-versed in certain things," Ufanari said.

"I had a good teacher."

The wind was now icy. Yet she had not taken an extra cloak for herself. Ufanari was not from the north so was well wrapped.

"From your look, you seem to be from the very southern shores," she said, as they followed her trail.

"I am. I married a Hyterta woman. She was taken by the Frekrikans."

"What happened? Why did they come?"

"It is not fully clear, but some believe the Krykarins attacked their homeland. They fled and met resistance here. So, they fought back and we lost many. Frekrikans are a tough breed."

"Did the acting regent not try and parley with them?"

"The former regent died, his son took over and is inexperienced. His advisors are not strong either. Unless they see a profit, they do not aid. Or so I have heard."

"I will ask further when we reach the capital."

"That will take you some time. Do you not have mounts?"

"No, we came through the gateway. The Frekrikans being here would also explain why the Shinra are so far south and in large numbers too."

"I hadn't realised it had affected them too."

"Yes."

He was surprised by the fact they had come through the gate. That city had been deserted years ago.

Now she had located the gulley and was moving along it to its edge. They were all huddled together. Quinn was in a bad way. She could see that immediately.

"You two, take the cloaks. This is Ufanari. Are you able to assist them?" He nodded.

"I will take the girl," said Tyca.

Before lifting Quinn, she wrapped her in the warmer cloak. Her skin was icy to the touch; any longer and she way not have survived. She gathered her up and held her close. Tyca was tired and Ufanari could see it.

"Let me take her," he said.

"No. She is my responsibility."

Tyca led the way back to the village.

She almost kicked in the door on her entry. It had the largest fire in the village and her friends needed to get warm quickly. There was a hushed silence as she appeared again. Tyca pushed past everyone and headed straight for the fire. She crouched with Quinn still in her arms. Ufanari was helping Marnari and Tullan to the fire. As they sat, Quinn rolled from Tyca's arms onto the floor and she collapsed.

Chapter 16

Several days later, Tyca came too. She had collapsed from exhaustion and the extreme cold. Even if she may have been from these lands and hardened to their conditions, but it didn't mean she was invulnerable. She came to in a bed, but had no idea how she had got there. As she rose to sit up, her first reaction was Quinn. Tyca pulled herself from the bed and dressed. Not sure how she had got where she was or whose bed she was asleep in. She was just weak from lack of food and a little dehydrated as she made her way to the next room. Marnari and Tullan were sat there.

"Tyca," said Marnari, "you're up."

"How long?"

It took a few seconds for her to realise what she was asking. "Almost two days."

"Quinn?" she asked, grabbing some water and the piece of bread on the table.

"She was seen with some of the other young ones yesterday, but…"

"What?" asked Tyca, sensing a problem.

"She has gone missing again. Ufanari has been asking around."

"Why aren't you looking for her?"

"We just took a break and saw you."

Tyca took a deep breath. She needed to calm down and focus. Then she grabbed her bow and weapons and was out of the door. Marnari followed.

Quinn had not exactly gone missing intentionally. She had been playing with some of the others in the area. The children on the street had reminded her of the capital and her time on the streets. Except these were just normal children playing in the street, not living in them. She had still been using Tyca's cloak and had taken it off as the others invited her to join them. The last thing she had wanted to do was damage the cloak as Tyca had been kind enough to lend it to her. She had carefully folded it and left the cloak on the bench that was outside the front of Ufanari's house. When she returned sometime later, it was gone. The other children saw her distress and could only remember a boy was near the house, but none of them knew who he was. The only plausible explanation was that he must have taken it. Why?

That was the question. Quinn had grabbed the cloak that Tyca had purchased for her. She knew that she had to keep warm and didn't know how long she would be looking for the cloak. The air was cold all the time on the coast line. Rhutra was a much warmer continent. Quinn wasn't used to it, but felt warmer whilst she had been playing. She had quickly glanced in on Tyca who was still asleep. They had been told what she had done for her and how she wouldn't let anyone carry her back. Tyca was a tough person, pride and the responsibility that she had undertaken meant a lot to her. Quinn knew it ran deeper than that. Tyca had felt like she had let her sister down in the past. Protecting and looking after Quinn was giving her a second chance, which was why it was even more important for her to get that cloak back. Considering Tyca's sister had made the cloak for her, she realised just how much the cloak meant to Tyca.

The mud at the side of the house showed prints leading around the corner of the house. Being around Tyca, she had picked up one or two things. There was still a lot she needed to learn, but she would eventually get there, if she spent enough time around Tyca. Slowly, the trail led her out of the village. Not good; she would have to be quick, otherwise the others would worry about her. It seemed that everywhere they went, there was something affecting or hindering their progress, although it had not been intentional for her to have lost the cloak. Well, it was looking like it was actually stolen.

Quinn couldn't remember seeing any other buildings in the area. That meant one of two things. Either he had been passing through and on his way home or, and she dreaded the other possibility. He was living out here. The wind was still harsh as she moved. The trail was less now as the ground was hardly touched here and was hard. Now she had to look for other signs, but she was struggling. All she could do was keep walking in the direction the trail had led. They seemed not to have altered once since she had left the village. Quinn wrapped her hands around her to keep warm. She could feel the courser fabric of the cloak. It was not as soft and nice as Tyca's; she could see how it had been tempting to take it.

It was at least another hour she had been walking and it was getting dark now. Not good; if Tyca found out she was here in the dark, after the efforts she had made to ensure they all survived, then she would be in real trouble. She either needed to head back now or find shelter. Quinn decided to keep looking, if the boy was out here then he faced the same problem that she did, although he had a warmer cloak. A track and trail appeared, it seemed to lead to somewhere. She peered ahead and it looked like an old mine shaft. Picking up a rock, she marked the nearest tree; so she knew the way back to the village. It was now out of sight. That was not good and if the others should follow, they would know where to look. Especially as she had just carved a large 'Q' into the bark of the tree. She continued along the trail until she reached the entrance. There didn't seem to be anyone there. Moving further, the light from outside was soon lost. It was too late to head back to the village now. She had been in the dark too much. Whilst in the tunnel of the gateway, Marnari had shown her a trick. Now she used it.

Quinn snapped her fingers and said, "Tulite."

At the end of her finger was a small spherical illumination of light. It would help for now. When she fell asleep, the light would vanish.

The light attracted the attention of another. Quinn had not ventured deep enough into the tunnel to realise that she was not alone. It was several moments later that she thought she could hear a scuffing noise. She waited a few moments and listened again.

"Who's there?" she called. "And don't pretend that you're not there, I can hear you moving."

There was no response. She had an idea, but was not sure if she could actually do it. The light was still on the end of her finger, but if she touched it, closed her hand or fell asleep, then it would vanish. Basically, once she had lost contact, she would lose the light. Still there was no response. She had to try and see if it worked. Quinn turned towards the noise and concentrated on the end of her finger, the light started to get larger. Then she flicked her finger towards the noise. The orb of light shot down the mine shaft. It was growing smaller as it moved and eventually disappeared, but not before lighting up the shaft enough to see the face of a young boy. He was probably a little older than her and had a dirty face, but she didn't see her cloak. She snapped her fingers and spoke to have the light return then walked towards him.

Now she could see him.

"Where is it?"

"What?" he said.

"The cloak. I assume you took it and that is why you are hiding here. I followed your tracks from the village."

She had slightly exaggerated that, but she had still found him so he didn't need to know all of the details.

"I'm sorry."

"Where is it, I don't see it. I was lent the cloak and it is very important to my friend." The boy started to move down the tunnel. Quinn held her hand up so she could see. How had he been able to move around down here? It was so very dark. Then she saw it on the ground. Her pace increased. It was only when she crouched down to retrieve it that she understood. The cloak was not lying on the floor. It was wrapped around a young girl. Younger than herself.

"Who is she?"

"My sister. I saw the cloak and thought it would help to keep her warm." The young girl did not stir. Quinn touched her brow; the child was ill.

"How long has she been like this? Where are your parents?" she had a lot of questions.

"About a week and our parents were killed when the Frekrikans arrived. We ran and hoped that we would be able to find a home in the south. I have found odd work, but nothing stable to look after my sister."

"There is nothing we can do now. We have no choice but to stay here for the night. Then the three of us will return to the village to get help and if you try to argue with me, I will ask Tybaris to bite you the next time I see her."

"There is no such beast; it is just a traveller's tale," he said.

"She is real and my friend," with that she settled down, closed her eyes and put the light out.

The next day, the boy picked up his sister and the three headed back to the village. First, she had to find her marker to ensure she didn't waste any time. In the morning light, she had been able to look at his sister closer. She was still sleeping and didn't look good.

"Why is there a 'Q' there?" he asked.

"So my friends could find me if they came looking. I'm Quinn."

"I'm Tura and my sister is Tiri."

They started off in the direction indicated.

Tyca had wasted no time and had rounded up all of the children in the village. There was some concern by the other villagers who joined the group, wanting to know why the children had been gathered. When they heard Tyca speak, they started to understand and realise. Some had been in the tavern that night and immediately realised her concern for the child and offered to help. She said no, if too many were out looking, they could damage any possible tracks or signs that Quinn might have left. Some of the children had seen her concerned about the cloak missing. As soon as Tyca heard about this, she realised why Quinn had said nothing to anyone else. The child was almost as stubborn as her. Tyca set off with Marnari following. Tullan stayed in the village in case she reappeared. Ufanari was also concerned and stood with Tullan.

It wasn't long before they came across them on their way back and was surprised to see she was not alone, but on seeing the young one, they knew why.

"I'm sorry," said Quinn, seeing Tyca.

"Not now," said Marnari, seeing the girl.

One look gave away her concern.

"We need to get her back, quickly."

Tyca was feeling more her usual self and took the girl then, she picked up the pace. It was a quick pace, but they were starting to get used to that. Ufanari could see there was a problem and opened the door to his house. Tyca went straight past him and placed the girl on the bed she had been using earlier.

"Everyone leave," said Marnari, "and you."

Tura had not wanted to leave his sister, but Marnari needed to be alone to work. Tyca led him out and he sat in the next room. Nervous and worried about his sister. "Ufanari," she called, leaving the bedroom.

Hc appeared from outside.

"I need brickle bark, sickle stem, and pollen from the lusnar flower. Quickly," she said, seeing him still standing there.

Then she looked at Tura. He was really worried now. "How long has she been like this?" she asked Tura.

"Couple of days, maybe more. I'm unsure."

"I'm guessing you have been through a brasnar thicket. Or something similar."

Tyca immediately knew what was wrong. The girl had been poisoned. It wasn't usually fatal, but she had not been treated straight away and so the poison had a stronger hold. The cold would only have helped to lower her resistance. When Ufanari reappeared with what she had asked for, she got to work. Among her things was a mortar and pestle. She started to grind some of the ingredients together with water to make a potent brew. The concoction was going to make the girl sweat. It was the only way she could force the poison from her system.

It was at least another couple of days before the girl was conscious again. Marnari and Tyca took turns to give the girl constant attention. The two were exhausted by the end of it, but the girl was well again. Some food and water aided in her recovery. Now there was another problem. The villagers were starting to get used to Tyca speaking and addressing them. The time in the tavern, the children in the street and now the care of the young girl. So, when she stepped out of Ufanari's house and called out for the villagers to appear, they knew to respond. Now most of the village stood around and listened to what she was about to say.

"Two children have been orphaned and need a home. I would take them with us to the capital and try and find a place there for them, but the girl is too sick. I ask for your help; will someone give them a home?"

Most mumbled, some made comments of having a family already. Ufanari did say he could help, but had no idea how to help the children. He had a trade to run here in the village and couldn't give them the attention. Ufanari had already opened his home to them and the sick one, even though he knew none of them. Quinn appeared and walked up to Tyca. She pulled on her arm and whispered in her ear. Then she walked forward and stared at each and every one of them. It took a moment and no one else knew what was up with her as she looked at each one of them. Some thought she might be trying to scare them into helping, but her gaze was moving quite quickly as she looked into each and everyone's eyes. It wasn't until she was nearing the end of the group that she caught a brief glimpse of a woman who had turned and was walking away. Tyca saw her pause and followed the direction that she was looking. She knew that Quinn had seen something. The woman had been by Ufanari's store quite a lot. She seemed a pleasant woman, but was quiet, even shy when you looked at her. Tyca went to follow, but Quinn stopped her.

"I've got this."

Tyca just smiled and Quinn left to follow the woman.

"Hello," said Quinn, catching up to her.

She looked across at her and Quinn caught another look at her eyes and smiled. The woman seeing her smile ended up holding the gaze for a little longer. It was enough for Quinn to look deeper and then she saw something else and her smile became larger.

"Would you look after Tura and Tiri for me, please?"

"I can't," she said.

What she had seen told her that she wanted to help, but couldn't manage the task alone. She was shy and timid. Never marrying, she had no children, but wanted some so much. Knowing that meant Quinn had an advantage, but Quinn was not one to push or press the matter. The woman continued her walk back to her place.

"Will you at least think about and consider it, please?" said Quinn.

There was a momentary pause in the woman's stride as she walked. When she looked back, Quinn had already left. Now she had to find Tyca, but first she would like to talk to Ufanari.

He was back at his store, it had everything you could imagine you might need for hunting, fishing, there were tools and even cold weather garments.

"Hello, Quinn. Find anyone yet?"

"Maybe."

She took his hand and led him outside.

"See that house out on the edge of town?"

"Yes," he said.

"Who lives there?"

"It is Milna. She hasn't been here long. I was one of those that helped to build a house for her."

Quinn already knew that though. Milna was soft on Ufanari and that was why she was in his shop so much.

"She likes you," Quinn suddenly said.

Glancing up, she saw Ufanari with his mouth open.

"You should close that," she said, "people are staring."

"How?" Ufanari started to say.

"I have a gift."

She then explained what she had seen and told only a small portion of her liking him. It was sort of prying and asked if she could persuade the woman to take the children, would he then help when he could? He could see that Quinn wasn't trying to matchmake or anything, only find a home for the children. Now she had his support, it was time to talk to Tyca. Neither of them did anything about it for the rest of the day, but it couldn't be left forever. They still needed to find Crellis and there was still a long journey ahead of them. Tiri was out behind Ufanari's house and appeared. She saw Milna and walked down the street to her.

"Hello," she said, "I'm Tiri, these are for you."

She had picked a few wild flowers and given them to her. Then walked away. With Quinn having lived on the streets in the capital, she had seen many things. Tiri had been part of her plan. Now the woman would have an image of her in her head. Milna saw Tiri return and sit next to Quinn. She decided to walk over. It was obvious what she had just done.

"You were right when you spoke to me the other day, but I am not in a position to look after two children. I just couldn't afford the cost involved."

Now for Tyca. She was inside and had been listening. Quinn had asked for her to be around today and to wait. Appearing at the door, it was time to offer a solution of sorts.

"I had heard that Ufanari would have looked after them. It would seem he has a big heart. Tura is over there helping now and has told the boy that if they get to stay, he will have work he can do to help. So, long as he does his chores and learns his teachings."

Tyca then took a single gold sovereign from her purse.

"If you decide to help and take them into your home, then I will give this to help and aid with their keep."

"I couldn't take anything."

Tyca nodded and understood. She handed the coin to Tiri and told her not to lose it and that when she had a home, that she could use it to help. Marnari recognised the sovereign and where they were issued from. Why had Tyca got one? Had she performed a service for that particular family and was now passing the reward on to aid others? She so wanted to ask Tyca directly, but kept hesitating. Eventually, the woman agreed, not because of the coin, but she knew it was right to try and help and she could see that Ufanari was trying to help as well.

Chapter 17

They moved on the next day, the two children had a new home. Quinn had told Ufanari to say nothing about what she had shared with him. He understood and promised to help. The group with cloaks and Tyca having hers back now headed north. Quinn had insisted that Tyca put hers on as her sister would be annoyed with her. They couldn't head west yet. There was an ice field, as they called it. It was the remnants of an old glacier that had found its way south and stopped. It had been cut off with a quake some centuries ago and eventually melted to form a lake. This at cold times, like now, froze over, but it was not considered safe to travel over the surface. Many had tried, but for some reason the ice only froze on the surface and not deep enough to be solid for someone to walk on. You could have tried to smash it and reveal the water beneath, but that would take too much time and effort. They had to go north and then west to get around it. After that, they would enter the pass that led to the central area of Hyterta and bring them closer to the capital.

It had been a long time since Tyca had been in this region. Very little seemed familiar now. Where forest and woodland had once been, it had all gone. One or two saplings existed, but it would take time for them to grow again. Their land had very little life. The northern storms had not arrived yet. When they did, the snow would come. It was unclear right now what they would encounter next as they were finding new challenges each day. Marnari chose to catch up to Tyca.

"It was interesting to see you give away a gold sovereign like that."

Tyca was no fool and realised that Marnari must know about the coins. They were rare and so would stand out to someone.

"I just happened to have one with me," she replied.

Her answers were simple and gave nothing away. Marnari could tell she was going to be hard work.

"You don't have more then or could you get more if you needed them?"

"I have one left and no, I cannot get more."

She really was hard work. They continued to walk. Marnari wasn't sure how to ask. Tyca never forwarded things and only seemed to care about the task at hand. Protecting Quinn and aiding them to find Crellis had been her key focus.

The journey was mostly in silence after that. The lake was frozen as Quinn looked across. Tyca had led them to it and then followed its bank north. It was an easy enough walk for them. At least for the length of time they had been in the village, Tullan had been able to rest his feet. Now he had to use them again. It was a shame that the village had no mounts they could have purchased. This was one thing that Ufanari didn't have at his store, but when asked, he pondered the idea for the future. It would be night soon; Tyca wanted to try and reach the canyon mouth before then. Her pace was steady for once, which surprised everyone. Perhaps she sensed no danger or wasn't expecting any.

They travelled for a while longer, took a break and then resumed. It made for a more pleasant day's travelling. Even Tullan hadn't grumbled about his feet yet. They were probably about a mile away from the road that led through the canyon. Tyca had stopped and was watching as other travellers were moving towards the canyon too. "This seems to be a well-travelled route," said Marnari.

"Once it would have been even busier. Something has caused considerable upset to the land. I will make enquiries before going to the regent's court to enquire about Crellis."

It was assumed he would go there, but not clear. They were behind the others some distance, but then they started to catch up on them. That seemed strange to Tyca.

She stopped and glanced around. Then smelled the air.

"Tullan, stay with Quinn."

Then she was off; she didn't run straight ahead, but to the side. With a gauged and calculated stride, she hopped onto a rock and then another, now she was on the side of the canyon. It wasn't high, but had been considered one as it would go deeper, but here it was shallower. Now she saw the problem. It was a hold up. The travellers were being robbed. She leapt from the wall; her bow in hand and arrow notched. Tyca had fired even before she had hit the ground, by which time, a second arrow was ready and loosened from the bow whilst crouched. She had deliberately not aimed to kill. They were Hytertans, the same as the travellers. Quinn saw what happened and ran forward. She gave no warning and Tullan had to follow quickly. Marnari had gone the opposite side to Tyca and had pushed the assailants over.

Quinn wanted to know what was happening. She was an apprentice and should always be studying things at first hand.

Well, that was her view if anyone asked. She didn't like being left behind and wanted to be involved. They were both her friends. When she caught up, Tyca was stood over one with an arrow on her bow aimed down at him while he lay there on the ground.

"You have one chance. Explain yourself," she said.

Marnari was ready in case anyone tried anything. Quinn stopped and looked at the other assailants who were now stood and waiting.

"They are all frightened and scared," she said. "Hungry too."

Tyca lowered her bow and offered a hand to the one she had threatened to shoot. "Thank you, Milady," he said. "We are all starving. Taxes have been pushed up and the capital is in turmoil. We had to leave."

"It seems the situation since I have been away from this land has changed a lot." Tyca went to the travellers to ensure they were unharmed. Then asked if they were able to spare some food for their assailants. They all thought it was strange, but she was not having them fight among themselves. All were Hytertans.

"We had hoped the capital would offer something better, but we can see that leaving our homes was a mistake."

It was a tale of woe. She was wondering who was acting regent. The one who had been in that place when she had left at the time of the great war had been old. She knew he had been replaced. There was much that she needed to learn, which gave her an idea.

"Can I ask both of your groups to join me and travel to the capital together?"

Quinn actually liked the idea and was smiling. Marnari could only look and wonder. There was something intriguing about Tyca. So many thoughts and questions entered her head and none of them made sense and she knew that she would get nothing from Tyca unless she wanted you to know. Maybe she had just left for war and had not returned as she chose to protect Tybaris. Right now, her thoughts were leading to a high-ranking officer in the Hytertan armed forces. Her skills certainly suggested that she had the skill and her way she dealt with people suggested a position of importance. She smiled to herself for the conclusion she had come up with from her own analogy.

As they travelled, she spoke with the two who had been leading each group. It was time to learn as much as she could.

"The current regent is the son of the last regent, making him grandson to the one who was in place when I was last in Hyterta."

"Yes. This one is a buffoon and as lazy as they come. He has replaced all of the old advisors and bought in those who are his friends and loyal to him," said Lorhan, the would-be robber.

"What was your function in the capital?" she asked.

"I was assistant to one of the former advisors."

"I see. That would explain why I nearly killed you and you failed to rob the others."

"May I ask who you are, Milady?" he said.

"I am Tyca."

Quinn thought the response was a little lame; it needed that extra fire behind it. "She is the shadow huntress."

The next step Tyca took was alone. Those on either side of her had stopped. The very reason why she had not said it.

Most feared hearing that name and only believed it a fable of old. Now they were face to face with that.

"We had no idea. There are many tales, but it is also said that no one has ever lived to know the huntress."

Quinn was curious, but needed to sort things out.

"She is my friend and protector and also protector of Tybaris. So, let's keep walking." Another tale of legends had been mentioned they had not realised they were in such esteemed company. Quinn looked up at Lorhan, she was really curious right now. "Lorhan," she started to ask. "What are these tales you mentioned about the shadow huntress?"

Tyca looked at her and gave her a glance, that she should not be asking. She didn't talk or brag about any of her exploits, but a part of her had also become curious.

"Well, there is this one tale that is told of how the huntress went riding in on the back of Tybaris and slew fifty Krykarins. It was said that it became the turning point of the war."

As he was relating the tale, a smile formed on Tyca's face, she was then trying her hardest not to laugh. Quinn noticed.

"Am I guessing that the story is not true?" she said.

Lorhan stopped and looked at Tyca too.

"Perhaps you would like to relate the real story. Or shall I pry it from you and tell it myself?" Quinn said, teasing.

Tyca knew that she could if she wanted as it would be at the forefront of her mind right now. She sighed and then started the true account.

"The war had been raging for about a year in the east part of Rhutra. They had been able to contain the forces so far, but General Icutaris of the Krykarin forces had taken a hundred troops to flank the Rhutran army. I had volunteered my services to aid them and had only just arrived and had headed across from Uboria. I was travelling alone on a steed that I had acquired at the Uboria port. It was as I approached the ongoing battle that I spied the General's little ruse. I charged the forces alone and cried out as I attacked. I was young then and an idiot. I soon learned not to cry out and warn the enemy."

Quinn and Lorhan were both transfixed by the tale. Even Marnari was listening intently, hoping to learn more about the mysterious huntress.

"Their warriors turned on me immediately and slew the horse in their first volley, using halberd. As the legs buckled and crumpled beneath me, I jumped and rolled. I had been taught to run and fire a bow, it took a lot of skill to run and hit your enemy at the same time. Their warriors were not expecting it. They fell very quickly as they could not track my position so easily. A moving target is a lot harder to hit. The General had already pushed on. So, there was only a small unit for me to deal with. Once they were gone, I had to catch up. They had already started their advance on the flanking position, but had not yet fired, it looked like they were trying to get as close as possible to take as many as they could and break their numbers. I was running as fast as I could, but the extra speed didn't allow for me to use my bow. I had slung it around my torso. As I favoured the bow, I had taken to using two daggers. I couldn't carry a shield so had learned to attack and block with both hands, if necessary. They obviously expected those with halberd to take out a single warrior, so did not expect as I struck from behind and started to carve a path through the lines."

She paused for a moment.

"So, you are aware. Tybaris didn't even exist at this time, but another did. I had been given an old relic, a horn, and was told that if I was ever in a dire situation where I required assistance, I was to blow once, long and expelling all my air from my lungs. Only would such an act bring me aid. I had not thought about it at the time, but knew I had to warn the Rhutran army. The horn had been bound to the one who came. I used the horn and without thinking of what I was doing, did as instructed when given the horn. After I had finished, I immediately realised that I had also alerted the General to my presence and a force of them turned to attack. I had chosen this path and so I knew it was my responsibility to finish what I had started. I attacked again and again. Never once wavering from the task. The numbers started to fall one by one. The Rhutran army may have noticed them on their flank, but none came to assist. I was vastly outnumbered and didn't know what else to do, but as I had been taught, which was kill them. I had slaughtered about half of them when I heard the cry from above. I had no idea until later that it had been the horn that had called him to my side. The black hawk as dark as the night, but more terrifying, was swooping down on my position. It was only when it attacked the Krykarins that I knew it was there to aid me. The two of us fought together and slew the remainder of the enemy. From that day, the hawk has always come when I called. However, that hawk is one I had met sometime before, but didn't realise that the horn had been bound to him. That is another tale."

Lorhan could see the horn was at her waist. Neither he nor Quinn knew what to say. As they walked, Lorhan tried to provide her with as much information as possible. Now he knew who she was; if anyone could effect a change, it was probably her.

Chapter 18

They made camp for the night, there was still more travelling to do the next day. Tullan had been pleased to have the extra company, more to talk to. Plus, Tyca could not make them all walk at her normal hastened pace. He had been further back in the group listening to the difficulties of those from the village on the north-east coast. It would seem they had all suffered at the hands of the Frekrikans. From his questioning, he had been unable to learn about the reason for the attacks on Hyterta. He shared what he had learned with Tyca. It was obvious by now that she had come from this land and the war had kept her in Rhutra. Or more precisely, being the protector of Tybaris. There was a question that no one knew the answer to; why? Why had Tyca chosen to protect Tybaris?

"It would seem the Frekrikans forced them from their homes."

"Did they know why?" asked Tyca.

Quinn was not here now or Marnari, both had been tired from the journey. She was surprised that Tullan wasn't tired too. Most had retired for the night and very few remained. Tilly was still around and Tyca asked her to join them, if she wasn't tired. She was the one leading the villagers, with Lorhan's account and her telling war stories, she hadn't chance to speak with her about the situation. Now she would make the effort if she had the time. She came over.

"I understand from Tullan that the Frekrikans are responsible for them seeking to travel to the capital."

"Yes. At the start they came and demanded we leave our homes so they could claim them, but we refused so they started to slaughter us one by one, until we left."

"They gave warning first. I am curious as to why they are even here. Do you have any notion why?"

"None. The only thing we knew is that they had several ships come across the sea and had landed in more than one place within at least a twenty-mile stretch. There are six villages in that area. I can only assume they all met with the same fate."

"We encountered two orphans from a southern fishing village who were victims of the Frekrikans."

Tyca was concerned, but she had no idea of the real situation in the capital. She would be glad when they were there. Then she would have to gather more information. The position that Lorhan had held could come in handy for her to be able to obtain more information.

Marnari had not slept. She was pleased that she had listened to the story. It only helped to support what she had initially thought about who Tyca was. The details she had revealed showed her much about her prowess as a warrior and how she had come to have the hawk at her side. She wasn't aware of who had given her the horn though, but perhaps another time she would learn that too. Now she had to escort the rest of these people with Tyca back to the capital. It would seem she was something of a legend to them. The huntress had returned.

Marnari was up early the next day and looked for Quinn. She had been meaning to spend each day giving her lessons for a least an hour a day. There were some questionable things about how she wouldn't engage in direct combat when facing an opponent. The two of them headed away from the group; it was best that she instructed her away from other people. She showed her several things that she believed that she should know. It was apparent that she didn't know where the style had originated from.

"I am sorry, but I won't intentionally hurt anyone," blurted Quinn.

She had been stressing this since Marnari had started to show her some of what she knew about martial magic. What Quinn couldn't grasp was that she could one day be put into a situation that would mean she had no choice and if she hesitated for even a second, then she could die.

"It won't happen," said Quinn.

"Do you really think I want that to happen to you?"

Marnari was angry with her. She had seen that Quinn was special, but only when she had been named Kokoran had she realised exactly how important. So important that the Frenaran alpha had tried to kill her. Even as a child he saw her as a threat. Quinn sat on the ground in defiance.

"Leave," said Tyca, who had been listening and watching.

"But…"

"I understand. She will get there in her own time; for now, find another way to teach her what she needs without killing. You can still learn a skill. I learned to fire a bow, but never killed anyone. Then when I needed to, I was able to do it properly and ensure that no one suffered. Try the same way, but not today."

Marnari saw some logic in what she had said. She was no killer either, but had done it. Her other problem was that she had not been versed in the style that Quinn had partially learned. Perhaps bolstering what she already had would be good. She left it like Tyca had said.

Quinn was still sat on the ground. Tyca went over and joined her.

"I spoke with her, but you will train every day and improve on what you have learned from a young age. If you really don't want to hurt anyone, then master what you have to the best of your ability. If you can show that to Marnari, then she will know that you are strong enough without killing and still able to defend."

"I will try."

"Sunrise each day whilst your mind is fresh. One hour's training. Now go and practice, then come and eat."

Quinn nodded and got up. She practised what she had been taught from when she had been able to speak. It had been a long time since she had done that, but as she remembered, she also remembered the old white-haired woman and remembered her words. Then partway through, she stopped. Pulling memories to her mind. She realised something and cried. The tears just came flooding forward. It was impossible to continue training now. Quinn turned around and headed back to the temporary camp. Marnari saw her and knew she had been up there practising hard from what Tyca had told her, but she saw her tears. Had she really been that hard on her?

"Quinn," she called.

She lifted her head and wiped the back of her sleeve across her tear-soaked cheeks and ran to Marnari. As soon as she was near to her, she wrapped her arms around her. Marnari had no idea what had happened to cause such a reaction. What had upset her so much?

"Quinn? What's wrong?"

"She never left me."

Now she was really confused by that.

"Who hadn't left you?"

"The old lady."

"But you said she left you at five," inquired Marnari.

"It was around then."

The two took a seat and Marnari listened.

"Whilst I practised, I went through everything she had shown me when I was real young. I imagined her in front of me and I remembered her eyes. Then it struck me, those eyes I have seen them many times since. A traveller, well dressed, was in the city one day and gave me bread. I saw the eyes, but never read them. They were the same eyes. Then the gypsy lady telling fortunes, she gave me a coin. Again, the same eyes. Every now and then I saw her."

"But you don't know why she left you to grow up alone?"

"No," she said, with some sadness. "At least I can remember her being around. Maybe not often, but she was somewhere."

Marnari ensured she ate. Quinn hadn't actually been sad when she cried, it was more to do with the realisation of the memories she had and the old lady.

The group of travellers continued forward on their journey. Tyca had seen the conversation and the tears, but didn't know the details. She just assumed it had been to do with the training earlier. Tullan seemed to be getting very chatty and friendly with one of the women who had travelled from the north and spent most of his time near the back of the group. Not wishing to disrupt his time, he was just asked by Marnari to watch their rear in case there were more bandits around. Now they were only several miles from the capital of Hyterta. The walls stood high and proud, but there were more travellers on the road. They were heading away from the city. It would seem a lot more were leaving. The problem was that they didn't realise that things were not much better elsewhere.

The group kept going; Tyca had encouraged the others to accompany her. She was hoping whilst she was here to learn and try to fully understand what was going on. Lorhan had given her considerable amount of information and Tilly had provided information about the Frekrikans, which seemed to have not been dealt with. The gates of the city were only a hundred metres away and Tyca stopped. Quinn was walking at her side again. She took her hand and looked up.

"Is everything all right?" she asked.

"Yes. Lorhan," said Tyca.

He came forward.

"Have you ever heard of a residence referred to as Forra?"

"Ycs. Who hasn't? It is a private estate on the north east outskirts of the city."

"Take everyone who has travelled with us and go there. If you are not admitted, set up camp outside. I will send someone shortly."

"Understood."

The group now divided. Tullan approached them.

"I was hoping that I could stay with the main group."

Tyca smiled. She understood why.

"That is fine, Tullan. It has been good to travel with you, safe journey."

Quinn gave him a hug and the three walked forward. It was time to enter the city. It wasn't as cold here in the central lands of Hyterta. The eastern coast had been very harsh. The land around was greener, but not perfect. There was a considerably better growth of trees, but as you glanced north, you could see the makings of a mountain range, blurred on the horizon. Marnari was not sure what other places there were in Hyterta. She had not been here before and she knew Quinn hadn't. For her first time out of the capital in Rhutra, it had turned out to be quite an adventure to get here. Now they had to find General Crellis, although they weren't sure if he still used his title. He might only be known as Crellis here.

As they passed through the city gates, the guards were relaxed and didn't seem to care who passed in or out. They were relaxed, too relaxed for Tyca. The streets were crowded and dirty. As soon as they entered, she could see why there were those leaving. It would seem that so many of them from the areas around had come to the capital. Obviously seeking help and aid. Possibly even hoping for a better life. Only to find that others had been doing the same thing. It was hard to move between them and make progress, but they pressed on. It had been wise for Tyca to have sent the others to the estate she knew. Already realising that much had changed, she wondered what the estate would be like now. There was one person she was hoping to see and find an old friend who she had not seen in a very long time.

Hubble had been young when she had first known him, but still older than she was, he had at first been her tutor and then in the service of her father. She hoped he was still around, now he would be quite old.

Her first objective, now she was here, was to make her way to the royal palace and get an audience with the regent. She headed to the one place that always had the local gossip, the Tavern. They entered and were immediately shouted at.

"She can't be in here," called the innkeeper.

He had taken a look and seen Quinn. Tyca was now wearing her own cloak, but when she wore it, her appearance seemed that of someone who was important. Her hood was up and remained so, concealing her features.

"She is with me," said Tyca, staring at the innkeeper.

She strode over towards him. Quinn and Marnari followed, but were cautious.

People seemed to be strained from the hardships within the country.

"Stay close, Quinn," said Marnari.

She didn't need to be told. Quinn was fully aware of tavern life long before she had even left the capital in Rhutra. They had also been in several on their journey here. She stood between both of them at the bar counter.

"I need information."

"Drink or leave," he said.

"Two then and water for the young one."

He gazed at her, but when she slid a coin across the counter, he didn't argue. When he had brought the drinks, she slid an extra coin, so that she could have his ear. There were several things she needed to know. She then asked, once she had learned of several things, if he had a trustworthy person who could deliver a message. Tyca had learned one piece of disturbing information, but needed to find someone before she made her way to see the regent tomorrow. The innkeeper said she would have trouble being able to see the regent. Tyca just smiled and said, “No, I won’t.” He let them have a room for the night. It would be a squeeze, but the town was full of those seeking help since the Frekrikans arrived.

Chapter 19

They next day arrived and they were up early. Tyca knew that she would not be able to get to see the regent until later. What she wanted to do was see the old city whilst it was quiet. It was hard to leave the room without disturbing the others and Quinn just had to follow her. She didn't mind, in some ways how she followed her around reminded her of a time past when her younger sister would do the same. The thing with Quinn being there was that she knew about her sister and a few other things too, having looked into her eyes and so far, had kept her secrets, but she was glad that she hadn't looked to deep otherwise she would know even more.

It was quiet, much had changed. Some buildings were empty, other places in need of repair. The capital was not as she remembered it. Seeing the city like this saddened her. It was not nice coming home after all these years and seeing what had once been the place that had been everything to her, looking like it needed more attention than she could give it. Quinn didn't speak as they walked, but it was obvious as they walked that not everyone had been fortunate enough to find somewhere to stay for the night. Many had slept on the streets and as the light was up and awake, so were they. It was hard to sleep in the daylight. Quinn knew all too well what it was like to sleep on the streets; she had done it most of her life. She was unclear right now how it would feel after sleeping in all the different places she had been in the last few weeks. When camped out, it wasn't the same as the streets, most of the time you had clean country air and the stars above. The city had the filth on the streets and someone drunk who might throw up on you if they had too much. It was a different life. The two of them returned back to the inn after she had been completely around the city. It certainly gave them both an appetite. Marnari was downstairs waiting for them. Once they had some breakfast, it would be time to seek out the regent. They needed to find Crellis and hope the regent could help. Marnari was still puzzled about Tyca asking for a messenger; who did she know in the city that she didn't go to directly?

Now they were ready and headed for the palace. It was situated at one end of town. On their walk they had not gone there. Tyca had taken a path that stayed within the city. There were no buildings on the short road to the palace entrance, but she did notice several guards there, more than would normally be posted there. Tyca approached them.

"We are here to see the regent," she said.

"He doesn't have visitors that have not already made an appointment."

"We are here on urgent business from Rhutra with regard to the death of the king. I do not need an appointment."

"Yes, you do."

"Then I suggest you fetch me the chief royal advisor."

They all looked at her oddly. Things had changed a lot.

"There is no chief royal advisor, only advisors to the regent."

"Then fetch me one immediately."

Tyca stood there unwavering. She had no intention of going anywhere. The guards had not been presented with a situation like this before. Marnari decided to step forward.

"I am Magus Marnari Rashna, I suggest you do as my travelling companion has requested. If you know who I am then I do not and will never make an appointment." A guard left to get some assistance with the matter. They were all new and young guards, Tyca did not recognise any of them. Right now, she still didn't want to disclose who she was. She was hoping it would not be necessary until she was in front of the regent. Marnari was surprised that she hadn't announced that she was shadow huntress, although unless you actually met her, most believed her a fable like Tybaris.

An advisor arrived, she immediately noticed that he was young and looked very inexperienced.

"Who are you?" he asked.

"We are from Rhutra and here to see the regent regarding the king's assassination," said Marnari, taking the lead now.

"And who is this?" he said, looking down at Quinn.

"Apprentice magus to Marnari Rashna, who stands before you," said Quinn. He then glanced at Tyca.

Quinn responded again, "She is our protector."

He was familiar with the order of magi, but was unsure if the regent would see them. Right now, he was in an awkward position, but knew that to detain them would be an insult.

"Follow me, but don't expect a long audience."

Tyca would not need a long one, she just needed long enough. The group followed closely and were taken to the royal throne room. Whoever this regent was showed no respect for the crown. He sat slouched and with his legs draped over the side arm of the throne.

A message had reached one particular individual. Hubble had come to the palace, but no one had been able to verify why he had received a message to be there. Unsure why and knowing that it must be important for someone, as it had expressly stated that he should not be late and he would be required. Hubble never liked to let anyone down, but whoever it was had obviously not yet arrived. He now saw a woman, a girl and someone shrouded in a hooded cloak. Their face was not clear, but something was familiar about the cloak. Right now, though, he just couldn't think what. He was getting old and sometimes it took a while to remember things.

Marnari approached the throne. Quinn was close by, while Tyca hung back. She wanted to watch.

"Regent, we come on extremely urgent business and hope that you would be able to help and provide us with information."

"Yes, yes," he said, "what is it you need?"

"We have come seeking the whereabouts of General Crellis, formerly in the service of the King of Rhutra."

He turned to one of his advisors.

"Do we know any Generals?"

The advisors looked vague at the question and the regent replied.

"No, we do not know any General. You will have to ask your questions and find your answers elsewhere," he said.

"Actually, Regent, there was a General Crellis here, but he recently left."

Marnari turned to thank Hubble, even though she had no idea who he was.

"Who said you could come into my court room?" blurted the regent. "You were removed from office."

Tyca was still watching and listening, Marnari and Quinn had turned to leave and had walked past Tyca. Her head was still concealed, but her eyes saw all. The regent was just an idiot someone who was lording the power over others, especially his subjects. It was time to stop it.

"Regent," she said.

He briefly glanced at her, "You're dismissed. We have finished."

"I think not."

"Have the former advisor thrown in the royal prison for returning and interrupting," he continued.

"Regent, you are an ass, a buffoon and idiot. You have no respect for anyone and care about no one either. The people of Hyterta need help. You are a disgrace and should never had been appointed regent," said Tyca.

Marnari stopped at the outburst and saw the guards' eyes all turn to Tyca. She had realised that Tyca had been upset and had eventually realised that this was where she came from, but now she was insulting the regent.

"Tyca," she whispered, as she got close to hcr.

Still Tyca remained where she was.

Hubble paused, that name. Then it hit him the cloak. It was made by… No, it couldn't be, but who else would have stood up to the regent and who else would have insisted on his presence. He knew now who had summoned him. Hubble took a knee. The regent laughed thinking he had stumbled and fallen.

"Queen Ca'Tyana. My apologies, Your Majesty, for not recognising you sooner."

Marnari paused, as did Quinn, who immediately looked into his eyes and saw what he was saying was true. Her head turned upwards. Tyca removed the hood of her cloak revealing her face.

"Hello, Hubble," she said.

Immediately, every guard in the throne room took a knee in acknowledgement that their Queen had returned. Tyca took a step forward and helped him to his feet. Then gave him a hug, which he did not expect.

"It is good to see you, old friend."

"I should have recognised the cloak sooner. How is…"

"Not now," she said, cutting him off. "Guards, arrest the regent and throw him in the dungeons for one month."

She then turned her back to him and looked around the room. Then she looked across at Hubble.

"Where is he?" she asked.

"Your Majesty?" he asked, unsure who she meant.

"General Gillis."

"To put it simply, the regent took his sword and fired him."

Tyca was horrified that the General of the Hytertan army had been fired; she turned and slugged the regent, knocking him from between the guards to the floor.

"You now have three months' sentence. Hubble, you are hereby appointed acting regent until you are able to find a suitable replacement. Replace and fire advisors as necessary. Would you also have someone go to the Forra? I have people there that I have given sanctuary to and ensure they are treated well."

"I am afraid that the regent took it as his home."

"Add another month to his sentence. For every citizen who makes a complaint about the former regent, add one day to his sentence. If he reaches five years, send him to Istgaard."

The guards were dragging him out as she spoke. Marnari wasn't sure if her heart had restarted, because she thought it had stopped when she heard that she had been in the company of the Queen of Hyterta.

"I'm sorry, but I have never really liked titles and when I went to help in the great war, I changed my name. It was a game Isty, my sister, and I used to play when we sneaked into the city when we were younger. I am surprised you remembered, Hubble."

"Why didn't you reveal yourself earlier?" asked Marnari.

"If I had come here as the queen, I would not have been able to witness the regent in his true light," she then turned to Hubble. "Do you have his sword and know where to find him?"

Hubble went behind the throne and unlocked the chest there and returned with a sword.

"I am surprised the regent didn't try to get in there."

"He did, but I said you had the key. You will find him at Greta's tavern."

She laughed and then took the sword. Quinn went to follow. She couldn't believe that the Queen of Hyterta had been her personal protector.

"The answer to the question you were going to ask is she is fine, that is why I had not returned as I have been protecting her, until she asked me to protect Kokoran Quinn."

Quinn noted that she now had another new title to add to her collection, but which one was the one she should be using. Marnari found it interesting how she had just referred to Quinn. It seemed more appropriate than all the others they had been using, but it could also lead to her being known and place her in danger. She would need to speak to Tyca, Queen Ca'Tyana about that.

"You stay with Marnari. I have to do this alone."

She then strode down the length of the throne room; as she left, the two guards nearby were asked to follow her.

Her hood remained down now, not that she was expecting anyone to recognise her after so long, although she was sure some would. It would do the people good to know she was here, back in the capital. Tyca knew exactly where the tavern was. It was Gillis who had allowed her to sneak out of the palace just after her eighteenth birthday and have her first drink. She had been wearing the exact same cloak too. Her father not been impressed that the General had allowed the princess to get blind drunk, in a tavern of all places. Her father passed not long after and she was made queen. He remained her General and she needed him now as did the people of Hyterta. Greta was in charge of the Tavern and surprised to see a woman with a sword and two royal guards appear through her door. Tyca looked straight at her. "Where is Gillis?"

Then she understood. She pointed to a table at the far end, in the corner. A solitary figure could be seen. Tyca walked over and slammed the sword onto the table in front of him.

"General Gillis, you are required to report for duty," she said, standing over him. He was so drunk.

"Go away, I was relieved of duty."

She sat down opposite him and looked at him.

"Your queen needs you," she said, more softly and quietly.

He lifted his head, but said nothing. With her right hand she held the left side of his face, supporting his chin.

"I need you, old friend, and so do the people."

He was barely able to recognise her, but to his eyes it seemed more like a dream. She stood up and turned to the two guards with her.

“Take him and sober him up, then give him this,” she said, handing one of them the sword. “Then ensure he comes to the throne room.”

“How do we sober him up, Your Majesty?” one asked.

“Throw him in the ice lake and put a rope around him, I don’t want him drowned.” Then she went to leave and return to the palace.

“Hey, he still owes me,” called Greta.

Tyca stopped took out a coin and flipped a silver Sovereign towards her. “Your queen thanks you for your hospitality.”

The room went quiet hearing the word ‘queen’. Their eyes just watched as she left.

Chapter 20

It was now getting late and General Gillis had not shown himself yet. He was obviously in a worse state than she had realised. She arranged with Hubble what she required from him. Right now, she could not wait, he would have to keep up. "So, is she still alive and safe?" she asked Hubble.

"Meaning?"

"Charnal."

"Ah, yes and yes."

Quinn was sat in the throne room with them. She knew a queen and it was exciting. "Who's Charnal?" she asked.

"You will have to excuse Apprentice Quinn. She has a very curious mind."

There had been a long talk with Marnari and it was considered best that Quinn not identify who she had really been acknowledged as.

"Just like a certain sister," said Hubble, smiling.

Quinn had not realised that she reminded them both of Isty.

Charnal was Tyca's mount while she had been in Hyterta. The beasts lived over a century and were not found in the main area of Hyterta. What remained of them lived on the furthest northern reaches. She had one during a solo expedition she had when she travelled north. Her intention had been to see the beasts herself at first hand. She was only recently appointed as queen and still quite inexperienced. The storms had caught her and she had to take shelter. Again, that was something she was not used to nor had expected it to be as bad as it was. It wasn't long after her return that Isty had made her the cloak she now wore. Charnal had found her and kept her warm. She was a youngling then. Hubble had her housed at a private estate that belonged to an old friend a little way outside of the city on the west side. The three were walking there now. Quinn had been so curious that she had insisted on joining them. She did, however, ensure that Marnari knew where she was.

"Jinra," called Hubble.

His old friend appeared from behind one of the buildings.

"Hello," said Tyca. "I believe you have been looking after a mount for me."

Jinra had only been looking after one mount. It took him a moment to realise who was stood in front of him.

"Your Majesty," he said, bowing.

"Don't ever bow," she said, making him stand up straight. "I have been away far too long and formality isn't my thing. How has Charnal been?"

"She and the little one have been fine."

Tyca was shocked and surprised at his words.

"Little one?"

Hubble explained that when the former regent took over Forra, her home, Charnal had been mistreated and bolted from the estate. He believed that she had returned to her home in the north before returning. They had found her asleep on the point. It was a place that Tyca and Charnal sometimes went. It was a peak that overlooked the frozen lake.

Jinra led them to the stables. There were indeed two Granos in the stables. The Granos was a large six-legged beast, heavily furred and exceptionally fast. It had a small face with short tufts of fur on the edges, deep blue eyes and a small nose and mouth. Tyca entered alone.

"Hello, Charnal."

The beast lifted its head and walked towards her. Its shoulder height was almost in line with Tyca's head. A large beast. It sniffed the air; the voice was familiar. Then it let out a low soft mewing sound and stepped towards her. Charnal then rubbed the side of her head against hers. Tyca wrapped her arms around her and hugged her. "I have missed you, Charnal."

Then she heard another mewing sound. A second beast had been in the stables too, lying down on the ground in the next stall. It stood, the beast wasn't as tall, but it took decades for a Granos to be fully grown. This was a male one. She knew instantly as the ears were always larger. It looked strong too. Charnal turned and mewed at the beast, it responded and then rubbed its head against its mother. Then, it did something that Tyca had not expected. It lowered its front right leg as if bowing and waited.

"Quinn," called Tyca. "Come forward, he is offering himself. Will you accept him as yours? I cannot own two, I have Charnal, but I cannot leave him like that either."

"How do I accept him?"

She so wanted one having seen the beasts. They looked amazing.

"Crouch to match his position and rub the left side of your face against his. If he accepts you then he will respond, then you can hug him, until he mews. That is the final acceptance."

Hubble and Jinra had never seen this before. Tyca had to learn it before Charnal fully accepted her. They all watched as Quinn did as instructed. It was a few moments as the bonding took place.

"Now you can give him a name," said Tyca.

"Shinira."

Now Tyca saddled Charnal.

"Did you really think I wanted to replace you?" she said, as she prepared her for travel.

There was much ground to cover. Hubble had people asking about General Crellis and believed he had left Hyterta, but required final confirmation. He had been very busy since being appointed the acting regent. He had no intention of letting her down.

"Who has the messengers?" she asked as she led Charnal from the stable.

"I do," said Jinra. "It was thought they should he here."

The messengers were Veron, a small fast bird.

"Hubble, despatch them, but keep some, we may need them when you confirm what you have learnt. Let all major towns know that I still live and you are now regent; it should help their spirits and give them hope."

"Milady," he said. He hated not calling her by her correct title, but years ago she had accepted Milady. It was less royal.

"Can I stay here with Shinira?" asked Quinn.

"If Jinra has no problem, but you will need a saddle made, the beast is too quick to ride bareback," then she turned to

Hubble, "I expect Gillis to follow, but I cannot wait, there is still too much to do and we need to find Crellis."

"I understand, I have the details you left me."

Tyca mounted. Pulling on the reins, Charnal was off. She hadn't run in a long time. The Granos loved to run and Charnal needed to run and she did, like the wind, racing across the land. They were intelligent and as she had a son and had introduced him to Tyca and he offered himself as a replacement. It was the Granos way, but Tyca was having none of that. She had learned about the Granos from a northern village, who knew about the beasts.

"Charnal north-east, find the Frekrikans."

There was much to do for all concerned. Marnari was preparing to leave again and Quinn now had another mount, but she knew that this one would not be able to leave the cold land. It would be too warm to survive anywhere else, but at least she would have another beast to ride when she came here. For now, she would enjoy the time she had with Shinira.

It was only a day's ride using a Granos to reach where she needed to be. The ride had been good for her. Tyca was more at home in the cold, but her duty and responsibility to Tybaris had kept her away; when she could, she would return to be at Tybaris' side. She dismounted and walked to the outer perimeter of the first village that they arrived at. Charnal stood some distance behind. She left her where she was so she would not be in danger, because she knew that if threatened, she would fight. Tyca approached the village. The cloaked hood was up. It helped for her to watch others without them knowing who she was. Eyes had been on her for some time now. She stopped about fifty metres from the village, her bow was in her left hand and an arrow in her right, but she remained calm.

"Who leads here?" she called out.

There were guards and she knew they were well-armed, but it didn't bother her. Several more Frekrikans appeared. They were all shaggy-haired and bearded. Really rough in appearance, but otherwise not dissimilar to her. They too liked the cold, but lived on islands to the north-east. One stopped and went to raise a bow. Before he could even raise it high enough to fire, an arrow appeared in its wooden frame. By the time he looked at her, she already had another arrow in place.

"The next one is through your eye if you attempt that again. I came here in peace, you are the invaders. Now, who is your leader?"

"I am," came the voice, as one stepped through the mob.

He was taller and had a thicker build.

"We have claimed this land and ask that you leave."

Tyca took several paces forward to make a point and then lowered her hood.

"I am Queen Ca'Tyana and you have invaded my home. You will leave or you will die. It is that simple. If you had come and asked for aid, I might have given it, but you have taken lives. I should have come here today with the intention of wiping you all out. Believe me, it has crossed my mind many times since learning of your presence. So, consider this your only warning."

"You are one person and there is no way you could take us all."

She then remembered something that had been said the other week and smiled. The leader saw it and was curious why she smiled. Tyca could see that the others around him were preparing.

"Are you familiar with one called the shadow huntress?"

"I am. A vicious, formidable warrior. Now she would give cause for concern." Tyca looked at him and met his eyes and then smiled, she said nothing more. "General Gillis will be here shortly with the Hytertan forces. You will leave."

"Gillis. He is no General, he was removed by the regent."

Tyca had held a hand out and Charnal had moved forward and she was about to mount.

"The regent has been fired and I have reinstated General Gillis, believe me he is on his way. I may have been away for a while, but it never meant that I didn't care about those here."

She climbed up onto Charnal.

"Remember," she said, before turning to leave. "You have been warned." Then she pulled on Charnal's reins and was gone.

It was about a half day's ride before she encountered Gillis and the Hytertan forces. She pulled up and stopped seeing the army coming towards her. They didn't have Granos. They had the standard mount, a two-legged mammalian beast, with a long neck and small head, that was not as quick, but moved fast enough.

"I see they got you sober," she said.

"I cannot believe you told them to throw me in the lake."

She smiled, "Just be glad I told them to tie you to a rope first."

He sighed and couldn't help but smile back. It had been a while since he had seen her.

"Oh, I have told Greta never to serve you again and never leave my army again without consulting me first. Is that understood?"

"Yes, Milady," he replied, then it hit him. "No drink."

"Consider that your punishment for taking time off. I had considered the stocks in the square, but other matters required your immediate attention. I had to dismiss that idea. I have given them fair warning and the consequences if they don't heed my words. They are all yours."

Then she rode off. She needed to get back to the palace.

Quinn was still at the estate with Jinra and Shinira. Hubble had returned and was in the throne room, but he chose not to sit on the throne; he had a table and several chairs brought in. For him, that was more an appropriate way for the regent to act. He had several squires with him right now. Giving them instructions on the use of the messengers and to ensure the birds left today. Then they were dismissed. Marnari was with him too. Between him dealing with matters, they were still sorting out the Crellis situation. Gillis had been able to provide some information that had helped a lot. The two, both being Generals, had spent time together, mostly at Greta's. He had come to learn of the king's death and had rushed off almost immediately, saying he needed to find and protect someone. He had headed for the coast and ship to the western isles. They now knew of a location to continue their search.

Tyca arrived back that evening. Marnari and Hubble were both waiting for her at the stables. Jinra had several working on a saddle for Shinira. They had already formulated between them what must be done. Tyca was surprised to see them waiting for her.

"Well, either you have all missed me or you have news about something."

"Gillis was able to provide us with a possible location and we think his intention was to go and find the heir to protect him," said Marnari.

"Where?"

"Western isles, Milady," said Hubble.

"You will need to despatch messengers to Lanuk and have them prepare a ship for me."

She stopped seeing his smile.

"You've already done it."

"The bird has already returned. A ship will be ready for you on your arrival."

"Then all we need is a good night's sleep and then we ride to Lanuk at first light. Thank you, Hubble. When Gillis returns, I would like the two of you to work together to sort out the country and if you are unable to find a suitable regent, then train one."

"I will do whatever is necessary, Milady."